Steele Secrets

Andi Cumbo-Floyd

Publisher's Note: This is a work of fiction. Names, characters, places, and incidents are a product of the author's imagination. Locales and public names are sometimes used for atmospheric purposes. Any resemblance to actual people, living or dead, or to businesses, companies, events, institutions, or locales is completely coincidental.

Book Layout & Design ©2013 - BookDesignTemplates.com
Proofreading by Laurie Jensen – lsjensen@embarqmail.com

Ordering Information:
Quantity sales. Special discounts are available on quantity purchases by corporations, associations, and others. For details, contact Andi Cumbo-Floyd at www.andilit.com.

Steele Secrets/Andi Cumbo-Floyd. -- 1st ed.

Dedicated to the members of the Central Virginia History Researchers (www.centralvirginiahistory.org), who showed me how to save cemeteries

It is easier to build stronger children than to repair broken men.

–Frederick Douglass

1

Here's what I know:

Ghosts don't show up for just anybody.

When I was seventeen, though, I didn't know that. I didn't even really believe in ghosts, I guess. Except for that story about the woman who stood on a dark country road and got a ride with a man passing by. When they told us that one at Halloween in third grade, I felt my skin wiggle up my neck.

But regular ghosts, the ones that haunted specific people. Nah, I didn't think much about them.

Mostly, then, I was thinking about high school and what extracurriculars would get me into UVa, if I decided to go there. Oh, and Javier. Sometimes, I thought about Javier. The way his hair fell across his face, but not in that Bieber way. More Johnny Depp. And I thought about how odd it was that at sixteen, I was enamored with Johnny Depp when most of my friends thought he was that "old guy" from "those pirate movies."

Then, as now, I knew I was a little "unique," but mostly, I was okay with that. Having the world's coolest mom helped.

Mom worked as a therapist, a counselor, a shrink, a psychologist—whatever you wanted to call her—she really helped people. I saw it every day. When people left her little office with the big windows at the back of our old farmhouse, they looked lighter, more even. Sometimes, they smiled.

She helped me feel the same, even though I occasionally had to warn her about psychologizing me. Most of the time, though, she was just a really good listener, a big supporter, and a worrier. It's probably ideal that a mom be a worrier, especially when she's the only parent.

My dad died before I was born, so I don't remember him at all. Sometimes, I ask Mom about him, and she's told me what she knows—how they met, the kindness of his heart, how excited he was to be having a baby. But truthfully, I didn't really think about him much at all. Really, I didn't. I know that sounds like I was in denial about missing my father, but I wasn't. I think I might have liked having a man around more, but I didn't miss *my* dad. I didn't know him.

All that's to say I was a pretty normal kid until that day.

I was in the garden picking green beans after school. We had eaten and frozen so many green beans that Mom and I had made up a term for the condition—green-bean-free envy—but we also did-n't believe in wasting food. Mom having to raise me and get her PhD at the same time had been re-ally tough financially when I was little. Plus, Mom saw enough clients who barely could afford grocer-ies—she did lots of counseling on a sliding scale—that neither of us took for granted the food we could have.

So I was out there, despite the green-bean-free envy, picking the last of the beans and tugging up the dwindling plants with glee. October is about the latest a good regular garden crop will make it in the Virginia mountains, and these guys had pushed their luck right up to the middle of the month. Now, it was time they took their final trip to the great compost heap.

I plucked a bean from the last plant, and when I stood up, I was in a graveyard. Really, it happened just like that—I bent over to pick a bean, and when I lifted my head, I was in a totally different place. No swimmy sky. No motion sickness. No TARDIS.

Just me, somewhere new, as if the graveyard had slid in around me while I stood in our garden.

It took me a few seconds to get oriented to where I was, of course, and I saw some small houses across and up the road and a few gravestones—the words carved into a few barely visible.

I knew almost immediately that I was on Pleasant Mountain Road—I rode it every day on the bus to and from school—so I wasn't really scared. More puzzled. But not really puzzled about how I'd gotten there—that question would come later. I'd seen enough sci-fi TV to know that it was wise to focus on the where and not the why when thrust into these situations. You never knew what might be coming at you next.

Green bean still clutched in my left hand, I stood there and looked around. I was just about a half-mile from home, and I knew this bend in the road well. Sometimes in the evenings, Mom and I walked this stretch. But I didn't know there were graves here. Didn't even understand why that might be the case. Most of the cemeteries I knew stood beside churches or behind big walls and iron gates. I'd never seen one just in the middle of a field like this.

I was standing there, slowly turning in circles when I smelled pipe smoke. That sweet smell that made my friend Amy's basement so special because her dad smoked that pipe. I loved that smell.

But Amy's dad wasn't around here. In fact, I couldn't see anyone anywhere. Walking a few feet toward the road, I kept turning my head, trying to find the source of the smell. I even looked behind some of the tall trees—oaks? Walnuts? But no one was there.

So I took a seat amongst the stones. I realized that some people might find that disrespectful or even creepy, but I liked graveyards. They were always quiet, and they told stories. Names and dates, and sometimes little messages that showed how much someone was loved, or how other people thought of them: "Beloved angel","Wife of." I didn't like the "wife of's" much.

I leaned back against a big rock—one that looked like it had just been plucked from the field over a ways. I didn't see any words on it, but I still thought it was a gravestone. It was lined up with a bunch of others . . . and some smaller stones were in a row about six feet away.

I was pondering the graves and wondering if I might need to walk on back home when he appeared in front of me.

I stood up quickly, part from fear, part from startle, part from training—it's always polite to stand when an older person enters. I felt my heart pound against the back of my ribs and clenched my fists at my sides.

At first, I thought he was just some guy who had wandered up the road and into the graveyard. I was old enough and had enough friends who had been in risky situations with men to know this could be bad news—a strange man coming up to me in a deserted graveyard on a quiet, country road. I felt my feet spread apart—ready to fight or to run, I couldn't tell you. I didn't take off immediately only because of that training again—it wasn't polite to run from someone who wasn't chasing you.

As I watched him come closer, I studied him. He was wearing blue pants—like work pants but rougher, and without a zipper. They looked handmade and so did his shirt. The fabric almost looked like burlap, but a little lighter. It was loose, too big for him almost, and on his head, he wore a cap that sat back a little so I could see his whole face, even though the brim was wide.

Oh, and he was barefoot. I couldn't imagine any man walking up the road barefoot.

Plus—and this is the real clue, I realize now—I could almost see through him, not really, but. . .it's hard to explain. It's like I knew what was behind him even if I couldn't really see it. But I really couldn't see behind him, you know?

My fear quickly slipped into fascination because I knew, almost right away, that he was a ghost. I'd seen enough *Ghost Hunters* and *Ghost Adventures* with that obnoxious dude and his crazy hair to kind of figure out what was up. My heart was still racing, and I could feel the tingle in my clamped jaw. Now, though, the adrenaline rush was kind of like that impulse I had in class sometimes to raise my hand every time I knew an answer. Ooh, ooh, I knew what I was seeing—a real, live (okay, not live) ghost.

Here, I was stumped though. I wasn't sure what the etiquette was. Did I step forward and introduce myself?   Did I pretend I couldn't see him? My mom taught me to mind my manners and respect my elders—and this man was definitely older than I was—so I wanted to be mannerly. But somehow I couldn't find the words to introduce myself or the will to push my feet toward him and say hello. I just stared, and staring is definitely rude.

My brain raced from ghost story to ghost movie to ghost TV show. I wondered if I'd need one of those EVP things the Ghost Hunters used, or maybe it would be more like that movie *Ghost*, where I could feel him near and see him but not really communicate with him. Or maybe I was the Ghost Whisperer. I started imagining myself in all those great clothes Jennifer Love Hewitt wore.

"Evening, Ma'am." His voice was deep, a little gravelly, quiet.

I finally pulled myself together, stood, and extended my hand. He just looked at it a long while, and then I tucked it into my pocket. Maybe he was a germaphobic ghost?

"Evening," I said, my voice high with excitement. I had never once in my life greeted someone with the word "evening," but then, I had never greeted a ghost.

He kept his head tilted down, as if I was still sitting on the ground, and continued strolling around the graveyard. "Mighty pretty night."

"Yes, sir. It is." I looked up at the sky just turning that silver of dusk. I took a deep breath. This was my favorite time of day.

"Looks like we could get frost." *What?! Frost? Mary, you can't come up with something better than that to say to a ghost?*

"Could be. Could be."

By this time, he had stopped walking and was in front of me and a little to my right. He didn't meet my eye. In fact, he didn't really look me in the face at all. Most polite people, I now realized, looked into your eyes and then looked away when they spoke to you. This man had never even glanced at my face. But somehow, I didn't get the sense that he was being dismissive, just maybe shy?

I turned to face him. "I'm Mary Steele. Nice to meet you."

"I'm Moses, ma'am. Nice to meet you, too." He kept his eyes away from mine, over my left shoulder. I resisted the urge to sidle into his line of vision.

"Nice to meet you, Moses. If you don't mind, could you tell me your last name?" I could feel my face flush with the question. "My mom always taught me to call adults by their last names."

At this, his gaze turned to my face, and he squinted. I could see that his eyes were flecked with silver behind the dark irises, and wrinkles were tucked into the corners of his warm, brown skin. "Perkins, ma'am. I'm Moses Perkins."

"I'm so glad to meet you, Mr. Perkins."

We stood in silence for a few minutes, the silver of the dusk dropping into the purple of a fall sunset. Somehow, the moment felt right, settled, like I was with a friend. I plopped back down onto the ground and looked up at the man in front of me. "Mr. Perkins, I'm wondering if you might know why I'm here."

I saw a flash pass across the corners of his mouth, but just as quick, his cheeks settled back down. "Well, ma'am. I figure you came here because you needed something."

I thought about that for a second, and then without really knowing why, I told Moses about the green beans and my appearance here in the graveyard. "Then, I sat down by this stone and saw you."

He smiled in sort of a crooked way. "That's my gravestone there." He pointed at the rock behind me.

I jumped up and turned to look at the rock I had been leaning on. "This, this is your grave. Oh, Mr. Perkins, I'm so sorry. I meant no disrespect."

I spun toward him just in time to see him throw back his head and laugh. I thought he might fall over, he was laughing so hard. I put my hands back in the pockets of my overalls.

Then, he looked at me dead in the eye and said with a smile, "No, ma'am. No disrespect here."

"What's so funny?" I tried not to sound defensive, but I don't think I did so well.

"Miss Steele, you are the first white lady I've known who thought enough of me to apologize for anything. And what you apologize for is sitting on the ground where my bones lie. Now, if that ain't funny . . . "

I wanted to object, to say that certainly some other white woman had been kind to him, that not all white people were bad, but I held my tongue. It wasn't respectful to challenge someone's experience when it differed from your own. I'd learned that from Mom.

"Well, Mr. Perkins, I like you, and I try to be kind to people I like."

I reached out my hand again, and this time, he shook it.

2

Later, as I walked home from the graveyard, doing my best to make it in the house before Mom came out of her last appointment for the day, I thought about Moses, the way he'd said, "Have a good evening, Miss Steele" when I told him I had to leave. About how he wouldn't meet my eyes most of the time. About his hesitation to shake my hand at first.

It seems ridiculous now, but it was only after puzzling on these things as I walked that I realized Moses was, had been, is—how does one talk about a ghost's life experiences?—a slave. Once I understood, that fact seemed so obvious. But really, at first it wasn't.

I suppose that might be because in history class we really only talked about slavery as an "institution." We talked about numbers and economics, and of course we discussed the part it had to play in the Civil War—or as my third-grade teacher Mrs. Carpenter called it, "The War Between The States." But we never discussed the people who were enslaved, never heard their stories, never thought about them as, well, people, not just numbers.

I think we read a little bit from Harriet Jacobs in English class last year, but then, we were talking about the writing, not the history. And I knew who Harriet Tubman was, and Frederick Douglass, too, but nothing in school encouraged me to think of those people as individuals with feelings and experiences that weren't some sort of symbol for a larger thing.

So in that sense, Moses was the first actual person I thought about as being a slave. Even then, I didn't quite know what to think of that beyond the idea that slavery must have been horrible. But horrible how? I wasn't going to know that for a while yet.

When I got home, I opened the door quietly and headed for the kitchen. I could hear Mom talking with someone, and a few minutes later a man walked through the living room and out the front door. I did my best to stay out of sight when Mom's clients were near because I figured they didn't need some teenage girl noticing them when they were doing something that a lot of people in Terra Linda—our town of just 5,000 people—didn't really approve of. Here in these mountains, most people believed folks should take care of their own business, and besides, that mental health business was just a bunch of hooey. Those attitudes raised Mom's hackles, and they sure didn't make it easier for anybody who really needed her help.

Mom strolled into the kitchen and pulled out the pots to make spaghetti—a weekly favorite around here. I had already put out plates and utensils, and I was just getting the pasta and sauce out of the cabinet. We had our routines down pretty well.

But tonight, I was keeping my back to her as best I could, trying to puzzle through what I could tell her about my experience without giving anything away. If there's one thing hard about living with a therapist—and trust me there's more than one thing—it's that she's trained to use facial expressions as a cue for when to go deeper. I needed to be prepared before she dove in.

"How was your day? School okay?"

"Oh, yeah, nothing special. Just more clas-ses and more people skipping them, you know?"

I heard her "tsk" from behind my back. I had known from the time I was born that school was the most important thing. Mom told me that over and over, and she reinforced that idea by be-ing active in PTA and fundraisers . . . plus, she paid me for good grades. Some of my friends' parents scoffed at that idea, but for me, it was just a re-minder that doing well in school was a priority. I didn't need to be bribed—school came pretty natu-rally—but it was nice to know Mom valued what I was good at.

Besides, I was clumsy as a bear on roller skates, so it was good I had something to fall back on. . . so to speak.

We puttered through the rest of dinner— French-cut green beans from a can (my favorite, and a treat given how many of our own green beans we had in the freezer) and regular spaghetti with plain tomato sauce and lots of Parmesan cheese.

As we sat down, I decided a preemptive strike was best. "So while you were with clients, I went and found this old graveyard in that big emp-ty field down the street. You know, the one just around the bend before you get to the old store?" I figured if I said "went" I wasn't lying technically, and I avoided all the tricky parts about just appearing there.

"Oh? I didn't know there was a cemetery there. How'd you know about it?" She spun spaghetti around her fork and took a bite.

"Oh, I don't know. I saw some rocks in the field from the bus on the way home, and I wondered what the story was. So I walked around a bit . . . Do you know anything about the people buried there?"

"Not a thing. But I bet if you went to the Historical Society downtown, they might be able to tell you more. That is if you care that much." She was looking at me out of the top of her eyes as she spun up more spaghetti.

There it was: The tone. Mom knew something was up—more than I was telling her—and she was testing to see if I'd reveal more. But I was practiced at avoidance. "Thanks. I'll think about that. How were your clients?"

"Oh, good. Some hard stuff going on with them, but I think they're making progress. Except this one man." For years, Mom had told me only small things about clients, just elements of their therapy that she needed to talk through herself. I knew that she shared these things because she could trust me, and I never told anyone what she said.

"He says he keeps appearing in strange places without knowing how he got there."

I almost dropped my fork, but I hated to be cliché, so I gripped it and kept moving the green beans around on my plate.

"In fact, he said he'd shown up in that graveyard you just mentioned." She looked up at me. "You didn't overhear some of our session, did you?"

"No. I didn't. Strange coincidence." I couldn't meet her eye, and I knew she wasn't buying my line . . . but I just listened. That was always the best course of action when in a tricky conversation. I'd learned that one from Mom, too.

"Well, I have suggested that perhaps he's dreaming or having a hallucination. I've pushed to see if he's taking any drugs or may be sleep-deprived. But he insists that he's awake when it happens and that he's 100% sober all the time." She paused and studied her plate. "So I don't really know what to make of it, I guess. He says he's going to sleep over in the cemetery on Friday night because then he might get some answers. I think that's kind of extreme, but well, maybe it will help."

How was I going to get to that cemetery on Friday night?

It's probably important for you to know that I'm not exactly a social butterfly. I have friends at school, kids I talk to in class—and of course, my best friend Marcie—but I am not one of those people who calls hordes of people "friends." Except on Facebook, but well, that's Facebook.

And my mom is usually cool with that, realizing I'm kind of introverted and that my friendships are deep if not wide. But every once in a while, she gets a little nervous about my "socialization" and pushes me to do things like go to parties she's heard her clients mention when talking about their children. But I'm not really a party person. Crowds— especially crowds of teenagers with red Solo® cups—are not really my thing. Yes, I realize this makes me sound like a grandma. But it's the truth.

Yet, in this circumstance, my crochetiness might come in handy. I had a plan.

At dinner on Thursday, after we were done with our cube steak and both just scraping up the last of the sweet corn we'd frozen from July, I said, "So Serena Jones invited me to a slumber party tomorrow night, but I don't think I'm going to go. I thought we could Netflix episodes of *Lost Girl* instead. What do you say? Girls' night in?"

Before Mom even spoke, I knew it had worked because she tilted her head in that way she does when she's going to say something that is kind but not necessarily what the person wants to hear. It's a key gesture for her therapy practice. "Oh, honey, that sounds really lovely, but I'm going to have to spend tomorrow evening catching up on client notes. I'm so sorry. I'm just really behind."

I let my shoulders slump and sighed.

"So you should go to that party. I think you'll have fun. Is Marcie going?"

"Yeah, she'll probably be there, but I don't really know most of the other people. Plus, a slumber party—they'll maybe want to do my nails or something." This particular concern was actually genuine. I wasn't much of a girly girl anyway, but my fingernails in particular were a sensitive spot since I chewed them.

"It's up to you, but I think it might be nice."

I sighed again, careful not to oversell. "I'll think about it."

The next morning when I came down with a duffle bag as well as my book bag, I thought Mom might skip a little. She smiled and turned back to the counter to grab my breakfast. (Mom insisted on a sit-down breakfast every morning.)

"So, I decided to go to the party."

"I can see that. Ah, well, good for you." We Steele women, we did not overreact to anyone's choices— subtlety and affirmation were enough.

"So I'll be home sometime tomorrow morning," I mumbled between bites of grits.

"Take your time. Sleep in. Just call me when you need a ride back."

Oh, shoot! I hadn't thought of that. How was I going to explain that one? I'd have to figure that out later. I could hear the bus whining up the hill.

"Gotta go, Mom. See you tomorrow." A quick hug, and I was off.

As I lumbered down the driveway, I ran through my list of camping supplies in the duffle bag. Lantern, snacks, bottle of water, flashlight, bug spray, sleeping bag. That should do it. Of course, I had never camped out in a cemetery before—or really camped out much at all, for that matter—so I was probably missing something crucial . . . but I didn't really care. I had just sneaked out of the house, and I was dying—pardon the pun—to meet this client of Mom's.

The school day seemed to last forever—except lunch. Lunch always went too fast because that was the one time I got to see Javier, and any time with him was too short. Now, don't think I'm one of those Bella Swan girls whose whole world revolves around some guy. I'm not. I did look for his curly brown hair in every hallway, but I didn't go as far as some girls I knew, who found out the schedule of the guy they liked and adjusted their classes accordingly. Some part of me was rational enough to realize that taking AP Biology when I couldn't even bring myself to dissect the frog in regular Bio was not my wisest choice.

But still, I was a teenage girl, and hormones are hormones. Besides, if I didn't have someone to like, I'd be totally out of the loop for conversations with Marcie, who had been crushing hard on Nicole for almost 4 years now, ever since she saw Nicole dance in a ballet recital when we were twelve. I always thought Marcie's interest in Nicole was fascinating because Marcie was an athlete—star forward on the basketball team—and Nicole was, well, a ballet dancer, a really good one. But we can't help who we like, so . . .

Today, Marcie and I were both a little swoony since Nicole and Javier were at our lunch table. Marcie kept kicking me from her seat, and I kept trying to act like my shins weren't bloodied to a pulp. When she wasn't kicking, she was staring at Nicole. Marcie didn't think Nicole was interested, but I thought differently. Every once in a while, I'd catch Nicole watching Marcie with a level of intensity that could fry an egg. My theory was that Nicole was just a little shy, and Marcie was pretty boisterous and super smart. If I hadn't known the girl since age three, I would probably have been intimidated, too. I kept trying to get Marcie to speak up, ask Nicole out for coffee or something, but she was terrified. Being a lesbian in a small mountain town was hard enough. Being a rejected lesbian in a small mountain town . . . well, you see her conundrum.

And me, well, I wanted to be one of those liberated women who thought it just fine for a girl to ask a guy out, but something in me said that I really needed him to make the first move. I think that's probably because I just needed the affirmation. Goodness knows I'd been wrong about a guy's interest before. Don't make me tell you about that time I made this guy Sammy hold my hand on a church youth trip. The boy looked terrified, and then he never spoke to me again.

So yeah, I needed Javier to ask me. And I was fairly sure he never would.

But still, I gazed at him while he ate his mediocre pizza slice. He turned to look at me, and I blushed. But I didn't look away, and he smiled and winked. I thought I might fall off my stupid yellow stool thing.

That wink carried me through the last three classes of the day. I am fairly certain I answered "Abraham Lincoln" to Mr. Hicks when he asked me who the second president of the US was. Distracted, I was a little distracted.

3

Despite my wink-oriented focus, when that final bell rang, I nearly ran to the bus. As Mr. Tillman poked the giant yellow beast up the hill, I thought about jumping out and running—it seemed faster.

I don't know what I was hurrying toward. It was just after 3:00 p.m., and surely this client of Mom's wouldn't come until at least after work, maybe later, but still, I felt an urgency to get there, to get myself ready somehow. This wasn't a new state for me. I was always hurrying toward something it seemed, thriving on the anticipation of an event. The planning, the traveling, the prep - most of the time I enjoyed that more than the actual thing I'd planned all along.

I was hoping that wouldn't be the case today, but then I didn't know if I could really hope to "enjoy" seeing the ghost of a slave and meeting a man who also got transported mysteriously to the graveyard. In fact, I didn't look forward to that introduction at all for many reasons, not the least of which was that my mother had broken his confidentiality to tell me about his cemetery trips, and here I was breaking hers to meet him. This was going to be awkward.

Plus, there was the tiny fact that I was going to the cemetery to meet a grown man. I knew this was not the wisest move in the world, and I was scared—as evidenced by the fact that I had packed not only the pepper spray Mom got me the same day I got my first bra but also a kitchen knife and a big can of hornet spray that I knew could reach fifty feet. I really didn't want to have to pack these things, but I wasn't totally naïve. I may have been completely dumb, however.

Finally, Mr. Tillman stopped—as I asked him to—at the old store just down the hill from the graveyard. "Good luck on your project," he shouted as I jumped down the last step.

I yelled a quick thanks and jetted off to the cemetery. I'd told him I was doing research for a history class so that he wouldn't ask a lot of questions, but I had underestimated Mr. Tillman's interest in history and had spent the rest of the bus ride listening to him tell me stories about growing up on a little farm just over the mountain near Lexington. On another day, I would probably have enjoyed that, but today, I could barely nod and "uh-huh" at the right time.

As I rounded the bend, I could see that the graveyard was completely empty. I headed to a large tree— definitely an oak, a white oak (I'd googled it) and dropped my duffel bag in a corner, where it wouldn't really be seen from the road. I slipped the pepper spray into my pocket, made sure I could easily find the knife and the hornet spray, and took out my bottle of Cheerwine, which I'd kept cold in one of those little promotional things you get at fairs. My bag said, "Have the 'time of your life' at Lake Lure." We'd visited the lake when I was twelve, and Mom had gotten a special thrill out of watching *Dirty Dancing* at the place it was filmed. I found the movie a bit, well, dated, but I did love the water, and seeing Mom remember her teenage years was pretty awesome, too.

Soda in hand, I headed back toward Moses's grave and sat down. Almost immediately, I saw him walking toward me across the grass. He had on the same clothes as last time, but now, his pipe was sending up a tiny tendril of smoke as it perched on his lower lip.

"Hi, Mr. Perkins."

"Hello, Miss Steele, but please, call me Moses." His mouth pursed just a little when he spoke, but then he smiled. "May I?" He gestured toward the ground, and I smiled and nodded.

"Okay, I'll call you Moses if you'll call me Mary."

I saw his eyes squint a bit again, but he nodded.

I felt bad because I hadn't brought him a drink, too, so I extended my arm to hand him the unopened soda.

He shook his head. "Don't really eat or drink much nowadays. I appreciate the offer though. Thank you much."

We sat in a silence that was somewhere between uncomfortable and amicable for a while, and then he said, "Mary, do you mind if I ask why you've come here? This isn't really a place for the living to spend much time."

"Well, today, I'm here because I'm meeting someone. But the other day, I don't know why I came. I just showed up here. One minute I was in the garden, and the next I was standing here."

I looked down at my hands and saw my fingers still had the smudges of pencil lead from where I'd drawn a big swirly doodle in history class. "Do you know why I might be here, Moses?" I looked over and saw him gazing at my face. "You said last time that maybe I needed something. Do you know what I might need?"

He dropped his eyes quickly. "I'm afraid I don't, Mary. Sure don't."

After a few more minutes of silence, Moses spoke again, "So tell me about yourself, Miss, I mean, Mary?"

My mom was a really good listener, and I had my good friends, but there's something special about having another person just listen to you. Moses was really good at it. He nodded as I told him about school and about Mom. He asked about my dad, but not in a judgmental, nosy way—just in that way that made me want to tell him more stuff. I talked and talked, and even though I realized I was rambling on and should probably stop, I just couldn't. It simply felt nice to meet a new person and get to introduce myself as me, a rare opportunity in a small town.

I must have talked for a very long time because I heard the sound of tires on the pavement and turned to see one of those sleek sedans that are always in those rainy commercials with lots of city lights at night. The car was pulling off the road into an old road and parking by a rusty gate. It was just coming to dusk, that time of day when everything is a little silvery. The gloaming.

Moses had been listening to me for over two hours, and I had not asked him one thing about himself. I felt horrible. Still, I didn't have much time to apologize or feel bad because I recognized the man when he stepped out of the car—the guy from our house. He was in a suit again—a nice suit as best I could tell. His skin was a shade darker that Moses's, and he stood about six feet tall if I were to guess. He was thin but looked strong. I double-checked to be sure the pepper spray was still in my pocket.

I stayed seated and watched him for just a few minutes. I don't know whether I thought I might startle him if I walked over too quickly . . . or, well, I don't know what I was thinking. But after he picked up his bag and dropped it on the trunk, I rethought my sitting plan and headed toward him. Better to find out if he was a serial killer right away, I guessed.

He had his back turned toward me and was reaching for his belt as I walked over. "Hi."

He nearly jumped across the road as he whirled around. "Shit." He took a couple of deep breaths. "Who are you? And why did you scare me?"

"I'm sorry. I didn't mean to scare you. My name is Mary." I extended my hand, and he shook it quickly. There are few things less scary than teen-age girls with long braids, I guess. Plus, if I could startle him that easily, I figured he wasn't a sea-soned killer.

"Mary, what are you doing here, if I may ask?" He stood with his feet spread apart, and his arms crossed in front of him. Clearly, I was invading his turf.

"Oh, I'm here to see you." Had I thought for just a minute, I might have chosen another way to let him know I knew who he was. I might have considered that this could get my mom in real trouble, that it might make him very mad, but I didn't think. "My mom mentioned you'd be here. "

His brow furrowed. "Your mom?"

"My mom is Dr. Steele."

His jaw clenched, and then he leaned in close. His voice was almost a whisper. "Your mom is *my* therapist. She told you what we talked about in our session." The hiss of the s's in *session* felt like they were slicing my eardrums.

I slid my hand around the pepper spray and glanced toward my bag far across the parking lot. I could make it if I sprayed, then sprinted.

"Does your mom know you're here?"

"No, of course not. I told her I was at a slumber party." As soon as I said it, I felt the fear leap into my throat. *Good move, Mary. Tell him that no one knows you're away.*

The look on his face seemed to pass from relief to fear in a split second. "You can't be here. I mean, we can't be here together."

"Why? I mean this is a public place, right?" I felt relief flood my body. If he was nervous about this, then I was probably safe.

"I just . . . " He looked around, spinning his head from side to side. "Well, I guess since you're already here. Why are you here again?"

Right, more information would probably be helpful. "I'm here because, like you, I just showed up here one afternoon, and I don't know how I got here."

He tilted his head toward his right shoulder and pursed his lips. "Okay, let me get changed."

I nodded and walked back over to where Moses still stood at the edge of the grass. "Do you know him?" I popped my head back toward the car.

"Yes, ma'am. He's been here before."

"So he can see you?"

"Yes, ma'am. Isaiah and I have talked several times."

Isaiah joined us, just like any person would join a group of people conversing. "Evening, Moses."

"Evening, Isaiah."

Isaiah dropped his bag on the ground. "So Mary, tell me more about why you're here." His tone wasn't angry anymore, but he also wasn't sending out those warm, fuzzy, let's-be-friends vibes.

"Well," I sat down on the grass, and Isaiah and Moses folded themselves down beside me. I'd never sat down with two grown men in a field, but I was all for new experiences. Isaiah crinkled his forehead again. "I'm here because I thought you might be able to help me understand why I showed up here on Wednesday."

I explained the story of how I'd come, how I'd smelled Moses's pipe—and as if on cue, the smell of pipe smoke wafted by—how I'd seen him when I touched his tombstone.

Isaiah listened, mostly staring at the grass in front of him, and when I finished he said, "Yeah, that sounds pretty much like what happened to me a couple of weeks ago. I was running after work. One minute, I was staring at the sidewalk; the next I was staring at tombstones. It was the weirdest thing."

"I met Moses that first night, same as you. Then, twice more, I appeared here—once in the middle of the night and once in early afternoon. That time, I was just lucky my boss didn't notice I had disappeared from my office."

"After that, I just started coming on my own. Moses and I have spent a fair amount of time together." He looked over at the older man—Moses was maybe fifty, Isaiah perhaps thirty-five—and smiled.

I sat quiet for a moment and pulled apart a few blades of grass. "So do you know *why* you started coming here?"

"Nope, no idea. That's why I wanted to spend the night. I thought an extended visit might give me some answers."

"Yeah, me, too . . . and oh, that you might have some."

Isaiah looked me right in the eye. "You can't stay the night here with me, Mary. It's just not a good idea."

"I know what you're thinking, but no one is going to know we're here together. And when we sleep, I'll sleep far away, just in case, okay?"

"No, I still don't think it's a good . . . "

Just then, we heard the sound of something heavy coming up the road. When you live in the country, you quickly learn to recognize car sounds because they stand out so much from the other noises—animals, tree branches cracking, birdsong. But this wasn't a car. This was big equipment—a tractor, a semi, something big . . . and it was coming right toward us.

I can't really say why we just sat there and watched the bulldozer turn and churn up the grass as it barreled right past Isaiah's car. But we did, all three of us. Still as stumps there in the grass. I guess it sort of felt like a movie, like it was happening to other people. Maybe I'd just hit my overload for unlikely things—what with the ghost and the other people who could see ghosts and all. But whatever the reason, we just sat there as the dozer rolled up and moved toward the first row of gravestones.

As it was about to push over the first rock, something sparked my feet into action, and I sprinted in front of the machine—between that big bucket and that hard piece of stone, and started waving my arms. I'm not very tall—five feet five inches on a good day— but I guess my quick movement and the tips of my fingers caught the driver's attention because he stopped . . . just before toppling me backwards over the stone. A fate that would have then been followed—most certainly—by the crushing weight of tracks on my limbs and chest. I prefer not to dwell on that possibility, or really even on the impulse that made me forget all reason and jump up. Because, well, it all turned out okay, and "what ifs" don't really help much of anybody, as far as I can tell.

By the time the machine came to a full stop, I was leaned back over the stone, grateful for natural flexibility, and I was smiling. I don't really know why I was smiling—maybe because I was alive.

But the smile quickly faded, when a large, white man with a flannel shirt, trucker cap, and jeans slung low around his belly burst in the front of that machine. His face was as red as a July tomato, and if he hadn't looked so very angry, I would have thought him jolly. His face read livid rather than jovial, though, and I quickly wriggled out from beneath the bucket as he screamed.

"What were you thinking? I could have killed you. What if I didn't see you? Seriously . . . " He was advancing on me with his hands out in front of him, and for a split second I thought his anger might be made physical because he looked like he was going to choke me. But then, he pulled himself up, took his cap off, and ran his fingers through his thin, sweaty brown hair.

"I'm sorry." I nearly whispered the words.

"Sorry. I bet you are sorry." He was quieter now, but anger still edged his words. "Really, girl, what were you thinking?"

Just then, Isaiah strolled over, and within a moment, I knew his choice to intervene had been a mistake. The bulldozer man's eyes flared, and he glanced from Isaiah to me and back again.

"Sir," Isaiah began, and I could see his face wore a forced calm. "Mary didn't mean to scare you. She just wanted to keep you from running over the gravestones."

When I remember that sentence now, it seems a little silly, a bit obvious, but at the time, all I could think was "Right! Right!" and nod my head.

The bulldozer driver had moved past my presence in front of his machine, though, and he turned on Isaiah faster than I thought his belly would allow. "What are you doing here? What are you doing here with her?"

I felt my shoulders go back and my chin go out—my natural defensive stance that belied the tears that also sprang to my eyes. I didn't like conflict, and I didn't like accusations—especially the unfounded one in the Bulldozer's voice.

"We were having a picnic," I shouted, and as soon as the words left my mouth, I regretted them. An adult black man and a teenage white girl don't have picnics together alone in a cemetery on a Friday evening.

Bulldozer strode over to me and put an arm around my shoulder. I think he was trying to be both soothing and protective, but I just felt creeped out. I didn't want his big paw of a hand on me. I ducked out from under him and stood by Isaiah, not close enough to touch but in a clear sign of allegiance.

"Young lady, you cannot be here with this," and here Bulldozer paused, and I felt my jaw tighten, "man."

I stepped forward and thrust my finger in his chest, but then, I didn't have anything to say. No words of mine were going to make this situation better.

Instead, Isaiah—clearly the wiser, cooler person—spoke. "Mary, I'm going to go home now. I suggest you do the same." He paused and then, after what looked to be a careful choice, he said, "I can give you a ride home if you like."

I nearly cried with relief. I didn't want to be left here with this bully of a Bulldozer, and while I knew Moses was nearby, I didn't think a ghost could help if I got in trouble.

"Oh, no. I don't think so," Bulldozer said. "She is *not* getting into your car. I'll call your parents." He looked at me and took a flip phone out of his pocket.

"No, you won't. I'll walk home. I just live up the road." I left my explanation at that. No reason to give him more information than he needed or to help him find me later.

Isaiah looked at me carefully, and I gave him a small nod. He returned to the blanket, picked up his things, and got into his car. I watched him pull down the road, and then I saw his taillights stop just at the crest of the next hill. He was keeping an eye on me.

"Now, you leave!" I nearly shouted at Bulldozer. I wasn't about to walk away and let this man disturb the graves of all these people. I wasn't sure exactly what was going on, but I was certain that a middle-aged man and a teenage girl having a picnic wasn't the only suspicious activity here.

"What?! No, I have work to do."

"No, you don't." I climbed back under the bucket of the machine and sat down cross-legged. Luckily, I had a paperback copy of *The Turn of the Screw* in my back pocket (our eleventh grade English reading assignment), so I took it out and began to read. Okay, I wasn't really reading as much as pretending to read. I was turning pages too quickly for accuracy, but then, that was beside the point. The point was to show how rooted I was to that spot, and if you know me at all, you know me and the place I've chosen to read are not soon parted.

Bulldozer stood there a while, bending over on occasion to look at me below the bucket, and then a few minutes later, I heard him talking. "Yeah, it's me. No, I'm not done. There's a girl sitting in the graveyard, and she won't let me work. "

"No, I don't think I can just go around her. She'll just keep getting in my way. "

Then, I saw his feet coming toward me. "If I pay you a hundred dollars, will you go away?"

I didn't even look up at that offer.

"No, she won't take money. I'm not threatening a little girl."

I harrumphed to myself. I wasn't a little girl, but I appreciated that he wasn't going to threaten me, I suppose. I turned another page.

"Okay, fair enough." I heard the phone click shut, and then I saw Bulldozer's face over his squatting knees. He did not look comfortable in that position. "You win. I'm leaving. But you can't save this place, sweetheart. It's not going to happen."

I kept turning pages, but I felt a tear well up in my right eye. I hated losing things. Anything. Even an old cemetery. And I knew the man meant what he said.

Still, I sat still as he started up the machine, raised the bucket high into the air, and backed slowly onto the road. I watched him travel back down the hill. As he passed, Isaiah's taillights lit up, and the car pulled away.

Moses was standing by his gravestone again, and he gave me a small wave as I gathered my things and walked toward home. I was suddenly so tired.

4

It didn't take much to explain to Mom my presence in the living room the next morning. A stomach virus. A rather gross birthday cake experience. A ride home with Susie's mom.

In fact, Mom felt so bad about my ruined slumber party that she made chocolate chip, blueberry pancakes. My favorite. But try as I might, I just couldn't eat much. I was too upset about the events of the night before. I pecked at my food.

Later, I might have wondered if I was trying to telegraph to Mom that something was bothering me so that I could talk about the bulldozer—both machine and man—with her. But then, I was pretty convinced I'd played it cool.

I threw my pancake out on the deck so the birds could finish it and headed into the living room with my book—The *Turn of the Screw*. I didn't really like it much, but I was trying to read the classics. I just sat there, the book propped open on my knees while Mom went about her usual Saturday of watering plants and dusting. She had a very predictable pattern. All the objects on the living room furniture were moved to the kitchen, and then she dusted all the surfaces before moving everything back to exactly the same place. Then, the dining room, and finally the bedrooms. It took some time, but nothing ever broke, and we never found those secret dusty spots that show up when you just shift things from side to side.

By the time Mom finished the dining room, I could tell she was on to me. She had slowed way down, and her head kept turning just a bit in that way that showed me she was watching me out of the corner of her eye.

Finally, she set down the Murphy's® oil and her recycled sock rag and walked over, dropping her weight onto the edge of the couch. "Okay, what's up? Something happen at the party last night? Did Lucretia really have a stomach ache?"

I wanted to resist. I really did. I thought maybe I could channel Haley from *Modern Family* and just be snooty and lie. But I'm not snooty, and

I don't lie well. So I looked down, and she had me. That was all it took.

She took the book off my lap, grabbed hold of my hands, and pulled me against her chest. Yep, the safe spot always made me talk, and Mom knew it.

I took a deep breath. "Mom, I wasn't at Susie's last night." I felt her breath catch just the tiniest bit before she forced it to return to normal. She was good. All those years of counseling teenagers and their parents, and she knew that reacting could throw up a stone wall. "I was . . . " I had never lied to her before, "I was at that cemetery I told you about."

She flung me away from her and turned my face to hers. "You were where?"

"Um, at the cemetery." I was trying to pull back, but she had a solid grip on my triceps. "But I wasn't alone. Isaiah was there. So I was safe." Oh boy, that wasn't the right thing to say. Her eyes flashed.

"You met Isaiah there? After I told you . . . . " Her arms fell to her sides.

I just stared at her for a long time. I wasn't quite sure what to say, but I did know that "I'm Sorry" wouldn't cut it.

She spoke first. "Why were you there?" I could hear that calmness had returned to her voice, even though the tinge of anger still edged her words. She looked up at me. "Why would you go there?"

So I told her. About my first visit to the cemetery from the garden. About how I had so many questions about how and why I'd gone there. About how when I heard about Isaiah I thought he might have answers.

She sat there, looking straight ahead. When I finished, she turned to look at me and said, "And what did you find out?"

A wave of relief as big as Mt. Lookout washed over me. I had seen so many movies where the parent turns mocking in these situations and says things like "And how did that turn out for you, huh?" Or plays the guilt card—"How do you think I would have felt if something had happened to you?" I knew my mom had probably thought those things—I could almost see her working the words through in her jaw. But she didn't say them.

"Well, not much because as soon as we really started talking—he was kind of upset at first that you had told me about his sessions." She blew a big puff of air out of her lips. "But we had just started talking when a bulldozer pulled up."

"A bulldozer?!"

"Yep, it was going to push over some graves, but I stopped it." Seriously, someone should buy me a muzzle.

"You *stopped it*?! How exactly did you stop *a bulldozer*?"

I had gone too far to turn back now. "Well, I stepped in front of it."

If my mom had been a fainter, she would have gone over in that moment. Instead, she took a deep breath. Then another. And a third.

I told her about the bulldozer driver's accusations against Isaiah, about how Isaiah had left to protect me and himself but had stayed just over the hill to be sure I was okay, and about how I had sat until the dozer left. When I told her I walked home, I thought for sure that would do it—grounding for life was on its way—but Mom was too preoccupied with the other part of the story to really note that. At least right now.

"Why would they bulldoze a cemetery?"

There it was—the sentence I had been counting on all along. My mom was nothing if she wasn't a curious activist. I had her, and with her, I had a way forward.

"We need to call Isaiah," she said. She stood, picked up her cell, and dialed. I sat back down and started to read. The *Turn of the Screw* was suddenly very interesting.

When Isaiah arrived later that afternoon, he'd already been researching all night, gathering information about the cemetery, the city plans, and potential owners for the bulldozer. It was clear the incident had upset him as much as it had me. But before we could really get into what he found, we had to deal with Mom . . . and Mom was never an easy deal.

She asked both Isaiah and me to have a seat on the sofa, and I felt like it was possible we were both going to get grounded. I crossed my legs under me and sat back, arms crossed, too. Isaiah leaned forward, elbows on knees, ready. After all, he had reason to be upset.

Mom started to pace. "Mary, I am very disappointed in you. You lied to me, and you betrayed my confidence by sharing what Isaiah told me . . . "

"Elaine, let me stop you right there. Mary betrayed no one. She only told me what you'd told her. It was you that broke a confidence."

I leaned forward and looked at Isaiah. Was he really challenging my mother? I glanced up at Mom. She had stopped right in front of me, gazing at my face. But I could tell she was actually thinking about what Isaiah said. She sat down on the ottoman and looked at both of us, her anger gone and replaced with the furrow between her brows that indicated worry.

"You're right. Of course, you're right. I'm sorry, Isaiah. I should not have shared what you told me. I hope you can understand that sometimes I need to talk through my day as well, and Mary's here and—usually," at this, she cut me a look, "trustworthy. But you have my word, it will not happen again."

Isaiah leaned forward further and looked right at her. "It's okay. I get it. But yeah, it was a bit of a shock to have a teenage girl not only show up at the place where my biggest secret happens but then to know that secret, too. I was pretty angry."

I curled back into the sofa again, hoping the big cushions would hide me. But before I could say, "I'm sorry," Isaiah continued.

"But when she told me she just showed up at the cemetery, too, well, then I understood, and I actually got a little excited. Her story meant I wasn't crazy. I wasn't even delusional, as you had hinted. Something else was going on . . .but we can get back to that. First, I think we have to figure out what was up with that bulldozer, don't you?" He stared at Mom with an intensity that few patients ever held up to her.

I studied Isaiah, and for just a second, I thought perhaps he was looking at Mom with more than just a patient's interest, but then, he swung his head toward me.

"Mary, what do you think was going on? Did the bulldozer driver say anything after I left?"

I paused for a second to think. "He did call someone. Sounded like maybe his boss or something. Told him I wouldn't get out of the way. But I didn't hear him say a name or anything."

At this, Isaiah stood and walked back over to the dining room table where he'd dropped his stack of papers. "I found these maps on the GIS - that website where you can see who owns what land— and it looks like the school district owns the land where the cemetery is. It's a big piece of property— a few hundred acres."

At this point, we were all leaning over the table and staring at Isaiah's maps. "That is a big piece of land," I said. "And it butts right up against the high school on this end. See, there's the edge of the baseball field."

Isaiah was tracing the edges of the property with his fingers. "Oh, you're right. I didn't realize that the school owned so much of that space back behind the building. But yeah, this piece of property does run right up there, huh?"

I leaned in closer. "Last week in announcements, the principal told us that they're going to be building a new football stadium, marching band practice space, and field hockey field. I didn't really think about it, but I bet they are going to build back here." I pointed at the space where the cemetery was.

"That's right. I read about that in the paper. They just started taking bids from contractors," Mom said. "But that's public knowledge. It doesn't seem like the school is hiding something, so why wouldn't they just start building at a normal time of day?"

Isaiah had taken a seat in one of our dining room chairs and leaned his head against its tall back. "Maybe it's not the school that's trying to hide something. Maybe it's the construction company. I mean, if they have to move a graveyard, that's a bigger expense, so maybe they were hoping to destroy it before anyone knew it was there. . . ."

We talked for the rest of the afternoon, strategizing ways to find out about the bid process for the school, trying to find out which company might have sent the bulldozer, etc. By the time Isaiah left, we had a plan, and we needed help.

The first person I texted—my finger hitting the keys even as Isaiah's car door slammed—was Marcie. I figured she might have some interest in the local scandal, being a hometown girl and all, but mostly, I knew I could count on her for anything. "Big stuff going on. Can you come stay the night?"

Marcie's mom and my mom were friendly, seeing each other at Marcie's games when Mom came with me, saying "Hi" when they dropped one of us off for the night at the other's house. I'm not sure either of them would call the other to go to a movie or anything, but I did expect that Marcie's mom wouldn't hesitate to let her come over, especially if Mom explained what was going on when they got here.

Marcie's text came back just a couple minutes later: "Be there in thirty minutes. What's up?"

"I'll tell you when you get here."

While I waited for Marcie to arrive, I swiped the Facebook icon on my phone and typed: "Anyone know anything about a graveyard on Pleasant Mountain Road? Took a walk in it the other day, and I'd love to know its story."

About that time, Mom came back to the table with a plate of her famous nachos—chips with lots of cheese, black beans, and just the perfect number of jalapeños. As we munched, we started a list of people who might help.

Mom jotted down the names of a few town council members she knew and then started a long list of friends and townspeople with an investment in history—the Historical Society, the town library, a genealogical group.

I thought about my teachers—Mr. Meade, the history teacher, would certainly be interested. Maybe those two guys who did reenacting on the weekends? But I was stretching to think of them— I didn't even know their names, and they were really kind of odd, wearing their Confederate uniforms to school every Friday. I think they sat alone at lunch.

It quickly became clear that I was not going to be the source of a wide variety of assistance.

High schoolers just weren't that into history, but they were into scandal. When I started thinking about the people who might want to get in a good story, the list grew quickly—the student body president, the school newspaper editor, that girl who seemed to know everyone and told everyone what she knew about everyone.

By the time I heard Marcie's mom's minivan pull into the driveway, we had a list of about twenty-five people. Now, if we only knew what we were asking their help with . . .

Mom walked out and explained the situation to Marcie's mom, who told her—as Mom relayed when she came back in—that she'd contact their church, the largest black church in the county, and ask around to see if anybody knew about the cemetery. Mom thought that was a pretty good idea since it might be a black graveyard. She didn't mention that a slave was buried there, which was quick thinking on her part since I didn't know how we'd explain we knew that, given that we couldn't read any of the markings on the stones.

But I did tell Marcie the whole story, suggesting she sit down and handing her a glass of orange juice— her favorite—before I began. At first, she leaned way back in her chair, balancing on the two back legs, like she does when she's listening to the coach run the same plays for the thirtieth time at practice. But when I started talking about the bulldozer and the man who tried to make me move, she slammed the chair to the floor and leaned forward on her elbows. That was her "I'm all in" pose.

While I'd talked, Mom had pulled together some more nachos and a plate of carrots and celery with ranch dip—"It's not really a meal without a vegetable," and set them out for us.

First, we needed to find out as much as we could about the cemetery. I did what I knew how to do so well—google—and searched "old pleasant mountain cemetery" but came up with nothing. Then I tried "Terra Linda" cemeteries and came across this website called *Find a Grave*, where someone had put pictures and listings for the graveyards in town. I saw the one near our church and the big one on the hill above the park. There were also a few small ones near old houses, it looked like, but nothing about this graveyard.

Mom grabbed her laptop, and she and Marcie started looking up anything they could find about Pleasant Mountain Road. I checked in on Facebook real quick and saw that a woman from church, Mrs. Abernathy, had written: "Sounds like you're talking about that old slave graveyard on the Sutton Place. Might ask the Historical Society about it."

I slid my phone across the table to Mom and Marcie, and soon, Mom's fingers were flying. She searched for "Sutton" and "Pleasant Mountain Road" and "history" but didn't come up with anything. Marcie said, "Try 'Sutton Plantation Terra Linda'," and as I stood over their shoulders, we scanned the findings, ruling out anything to do with a place in Indiana, until we got to the bottom of the page. It was just a little note:

"Auction Notice: Sutton Plantation. All bids taken. August 19, 1897."

A quick click showed that the plantation and all of its belongings had been sold at auction more than a hundred years ago when the owners—Tobias and Jake Sutton—could not afford to keep the plantation running. They were selling furniture and dishes and farm equipment. Sort of an old-timey "everything must go" sale.

We typed in "Tobias Sutton" and "Jake Sutton" and found they were the grandsons of the original owner—Maurice Sutton, one of the wealthiest men in Terra Linda at the time. The Historical Society website had a whole write-up on him. Apparently, he'd owned almost one thousand acres of land along what was now Pleasant Mountain Road. He had made his money selling tobacco, and he was married twice and had five children, three girls and two boys.

Nowadays, if you saw someone had one thousand acres of farmland, you imagined big John Deere tractors and binders for hay. But then, of course, they didn't have machines to farm. They had slaves.

Marcie and I must have had the same thought at the same moment because we looked at each other and said quietly, "Moses." Mom was already ahead of us. She searched "Maurice Sutton slaves," and we got sent to Ancestry.com. I didn't know much about the website except that Mr. Meade had mentioned it was a good place to find out about your family tree.

Mom didn't hesitate to set up a free trial account and log in to the page Google sent us to. There, we saw the 1850 Virginia Slave Census, and Maurice Sutton's name was about one-third of the way down the page.

Maurice J. Sutton   1   19   M   B

The first column showed the number of slaves in that row; the second, the age of each particular enslaved person; the third, that person's sex; and the fourth, their skin color. Sutton's list filled a whole column and then some on this "Slave Schedule." Apparently, Sutton had owned over fifty slaves—most between the ages of twenty and fifty but with about ten kids and three older people—eighty-six, ninety-three, and seventy-seven.

I knew Moses was in those pages. I knew he was listed there—his sex, his age, his skin color. I didn't know which one of those little hash marks and listings described him, but I sure was going to find out.

5

It seems wise here to interrupt myself to tell you a little about what I knew at that point about history—particularly the history of slavery. My teachers had often talked about slavery, especially during Black History Month, but the conversation was usually very general. We had some dates—The Civil War, The Emancipation Proclamation—and the most ambitious of teachers sometimes played a recording of Lincoln's famous speech at Gettysburg. We talked about some general ideas of evil, about how slavery meant that people owned other people, about freedom—a concept that is almost impossible for most American humans, let alone most American children, to conceive of. We may

have read a little bit of the Harriets: Tubman, Jacobs, Beecher Stowe. But that was about it.

We didn't learn about the laws around slavery— how debilitating and complex they were. We
didn't talk about whippings or the sale of children.
We certainly didn't bring up rape. The hard stuff
was strictly off limits—reserved for our parents or
researchers—too risky to bring up in class, even
though we saw pictures of the Hiroshima bomb-
ings every year, so that rationale really made no
sense.

But we didn't learn more innocuous stuff either. I didn't know what kind of houses slaves
lived in or anything about what they ate. I didn't
hear about what kind of work they did, and I certainly wasn't aware of differences from plantation
to plantation. Nope, slavery was just this big, ab-
stract, bad thing that happened to black people.
And thus, it wasn't very real at all.

Before you get all defensive on behalf of
teachers and testing and the time available to them,
let me just stop you right there. I love teachers,
and I'm not really faulting them. They do have
tests to prep for, and they do have limited time.
Plus, they probably weren't taught much about
slavery either, so how could they teach us? But I
will bring up this one point . . . At five, I could tell
you what kinds of dinosaurs once inhabited North
America. I could tell you the basic difference be-

tween the types of housing that various tribes of American Indians lived in by the time I was eight. And in tenth grade, I had memorized the Bill of Rights . . . so if I had time to learn about these parts of American history—important parts, too—then surely we had more time to talk about slavery in a real way—in a way that included people's names and stories about their daily lives. Seems like there was a little intentional glazing over here . . . at least that's how I see it now, now that Moses is my friend.

All that is to say that I didn't really have any context for what was going on when Moses had been alive. I did, however, know what today looked like— what Shamila called "the legacy of racism." Shamila was the woman I met that Monday at the Historical Society when I went by after school. Mom had decided that this would be a good "extra-curricular" activity for me, but I suspect it was also, in part, a punishment for lying to her. At any rate, I walked to the Mahalland Historical Society right after school.

The building was old and deep, one of those houses on the main street in Terra Linda that looks tiny until you realize it stretches about eight miles back from the road. The sign by the door said it had been built in 1803 as the stagecoach stop in town. Since it was right next to the courthouse, I guess that made sense. Even now, it was really only the courthouse that got much traffic downtown.

Shamila came as soon as the heavy bell on the door clanged when I passed under it. She was a tall black woman with the most awesome t-shirt I had ever seen. It said "History Buff" on the front and showed a body builder flexing. I made a mental note to ask her where she got it once I knew her better. (I had no doubt I'd get to know her better. From Mom's tone when she reminded me to stop here this morning, I figured I might be spending every afternoon in old papers.)

I introduced myself and told her that I was looking for information about a cemetery up on Pleasant Mountain Road and that I thought it was on the Sutton Plantation.

She smiled. "I see you've already been doing a little research, huh? For you to know it was on the Sutton property and all. Let me see what I have about them."

She slipped into a room beside us and left me standing in the hallway. The house still looked like what I imagine it did back in 1803. One long, central hallway with a couple of rooms off to each side. Out the back, I could see what looked like a stainless steel refrigerator and right in front of it, on a bump out in the wall, there was an old map. "Hotchkiss," it said in one corner. I leaned in to look closer and saw it said "Mahalland County" on the bottom of the page. I stared carefully, and there was Terra Linda, right in the middle. I could see the rest of the towns around, too, and the rivers. Even some of the roads were the same.

Shamila came back with a green box that had a flip-top lid and said, "Follow me" as she walked across the hallway to a room with three big tables. Each had a lamp on top and was shiny with polish. She set the box down gently in the middle of the nearest table and pointed to a seat for me.

"This is everything we have on the Sutton family. At first glance, I think this might be what you're most interested in." She carefully lifted out a map that kind of looked like the one in the hallway. It was definitely yellowed and fragile.

"Please, put these on." Shamila handed me white gloves, and I slipped them over my hands, the tips bending at the end because my fingers were so small. With slow care, I picked up the map and held it close to my face. I could see Pleasant Mountain Road, and I traced its line with my eyes until I found the bend near where the graveyard was. I laid the map down and then moved my gloved finger gently to the right an inch or so, and just there, I saw a small cross. "Does that mean graveyard?" I looked up at Shamila.

"Well, actually that cross marks a church, probably Mt. Beulah just down the way. But this square, it could be a cemetery." She pointed to a tiny mark by the road.

I sat back in my chair and stared at the map from afar. That was it—a slave cemetery. That's why Moses was there. I took a deep breath. "Is there anything about the slaves that were buried there?"

Shamila took the chair across from me and spun the box back toward herself. As she slowly flipped through the files, she asked, "If I may, why are you so interested in this old cemetery?"

I didn't know this woman at all, never had laid eyes on her before that bell rang on the door, but somehow I knew I could trust her. "Well, I think someone's trying to destroy it." I told her about the bulldozer and about how we thought it might be one of the builders bidding on the ball fields.

It was only when I finished talking that I realized she wasn't flipping through the folders anymore. "They're going to just dig up a cemetery? Without asking anyone about it? Without even a public notice?"

Like I said, I didn't know Shamila, but even I could tell she was steaming. I thought she might break her teeth she was clenching her jaw so hard. "Well, if that's the case, then we have some real work to do. Let's start at the beginning." She pulled all the folders out of the box and laid them on the table.

I looked at her, and she lifted her gaze to mine. "Mary, we've got some history to save."

She took half of the folders and put them in front of me and held the other half for herself. There wasn't anybody else in the building, so I guess she figured she could spare some time to get me started.

Each of us flipped open a green folder, and I looked at the papers in mine. A letter. I could read the date—October 14, 1834—but then the rest was much harder to make out. It was handwritten, of course, and slanted really far to the right. I kept staring though, and soon, my brain started to make out more words.

Dearest Aunt Delilah,

The sunshine on the fields this morning is spectacular. Bright with dew and the first taste of frost. While the leaves are still a bit from bringing their best performance, they are beginning to change the look of the farm, as if preparing us for the starkness of winter.

Work here goes well. The servants have got up most of the corn and put it in the cribs, and soon, the wheat harvest will begin. It's a real joy to see them out in those fields doing what they were made to do, and they really are good folk. Obedient, kind. Millie, the house girl, has really taken to me. She sits most days at my feet and mends while I stitch my embroidery.

Father is well, too, if his usual preoccupied self. He has seemed in good spirits lately. I expect because the reports from the tobacco sales over in Richmond are good.

We hope with all our hearts that you will come see us soon. We know it's a long ride from Baltimore, but your presence here would add a shine to our day.

With all my love,

Yvette

I wasn't sure what to make of this letter. I thought I could probably like Yvette, but then, how could she really think a little girl wanted to sit at her feet all day and mend things? The little girls I knew from church wanted to run around and hide in the bushes and build towers and play school. I'd have to think about that more.

Shamila, meanwhile, had flipped through two or three folders already, and the notepad at her left hand was full of dates and names. When she saw me looking at her, she glanced up and then put her pen down. "Okay, so here's what I've got. The place was built in about 1810 by Josiah Scott. He had come up, I think, from James City, and he brought his wife, Lily, his daughter, Yvette, and his son, Josiah, Jr."

I told her about the letter and confirmed that "Father" must have been Josiah. Then, Shamila continued, "According to this inventory from December 1840, the Scotts owned two carriages, sixteen horses, forty cattle, two spades, one spinning wheel, some sundry dishes, and eighty-two human beings."

I saw the corner of her mouth turn when she said that last part, and I imagined my face looked upset, too. "So wait, the inventory lists the carriages and dishes with the people?"

"Oh, that's nothing. I've seen a single sheet of paper list enslaved people on one side and litters of puppies on the other."

I must have looked confused because she explained, "Mary, I know you know what slavery was. But this is the reality of it—people were considered no better than dogs in quite a literal way. The reason slaves were sometimes listed on inventories of the animals was that it was important to keep track of the breeding practices of all the "things" you owned. You wanted to know how many baby cows you owned, and you wanted to know how many baby nig—how many black babies you owned. The more children your slaves had, the richer you were. Understand?"

I understood the facts of what she was saying, of course, but no, I didn't understand. How was that even possible, that people could think of other human beings as property? Could care only about new babies because they made them richer? I didn't even know what to say.

Shamila reached a hand across the table and put it on my arm. "I know. It's hard. It's really hard. You're just coming to know it, or to understand it, from the look on your face. I've known about slavery my whole life. It lives in my skin, moves in my bones. My grandmother tells stories from her grandmother, a woman who was a slave right here in Malhalland. Even so, I still think I'm having some sort of nightmare."

I laid my free hand on Shamila's fingers and felt tears prick my eyes. I had no idea. I really had no idea about any of this, and I had no idea what to say now. So I just smiled and squeezed her fingers. Before I took a deep breath, "So maybe the cemetery is a slave cemetery?" I asked tentatively.

Drawing her hand back gently, Shamila tilted her head. "What makes you say that?"

"Well, for one, none of the stones really have any carvings on them. And now that you say these people were considered to be like dogs, wouldn't it make sense that slaves were buried in graveyards without marked stones?"

"That's a possibility, for sure," she said, "but it could also be that the stones were just old and worn down by weather. Right?"

Uh-oh. She had that same tone Mom got when she knew I was holding back. I leaned back in my chair and took a deep breath. Then, looking down at my interwoven fingers, I said, "Well, and there's   Moses."

6

By the time I met up with Mom and Isaiah for dinner at the pizza place in town, our "project" had come to involve a camera crew and a reporter, and I wasn't sure what Mom would say about that.

When I had told Shamila about Moses, she hadn't even wrinkled her nose. Seems she was quite familiar with ghosts even if she didn't see them herself. Her grandmother did, all the time, and so Moses's appearance, while interesting to her, wasn't really the crux of the matter. The fact that it was a slave cemetery was. That spurred her to a whole new level of action.

Before I knew what was really happening, she'd picked up the phone and called her friend, Beatrice, who was a reporter at Channel 28, the TV station over the mountain in Lexington. I could hear her explain what was happening—bulldozer, slave cemetery, teenage white girl—from the next room where I sat and flipped through more Sutton folders. Of course, I wasn't really seeing what I was reading. I was worrying. I wasn't sure TV coverage had been something we wanted.

But as I bit into my slice of extra cheese, Mom and Isaiah worked the presence of a reporter and a camera in as if they had been doing publicity their whole lives. They talked about camera angles and who should be on camera—"Mary, of course"—and I nearly choked on my pizza.

"What?! Me? Why?"

"Mary, honey, you're the most persuasive voice we have," Mom said in the soft, near whisper she uses as persuasion. "People will pay attention if a teenage girl is involved."

"A teenage white girl," Isaiah added.

"Wait, Shamila said the same thing, 'teenage white girl.' Why does it matter that I'm white?"

Isaiah put down the bite of spinach calzone he had been about to eat and looked at me. "Mary, it matters for a lot of reasons, not the least of which is that people will actually pay attention to you. If a black person were to speak up, suddenly the conversation could become imbued with a whole hue of prejudice and racism that just isn't useful. Many people would assume—as they often do—that 'we' just needed to get over 'it.' Plus, you as the voice of this mission will gain a wider audience. White people don't often listen to what black people say, but they will listen to what a white girl says."

I wasn't sure I agreed with him. I wanted to believe that race didn't matter that way anymore, that Dr. King's "content of their character" speech had come true. But then I remembered what happened when he and I were in the cemetery. Sure, any man and a teenage girl in that situation would have looked odd, but I knew there was something about the fact that Isaiah was black that made a difference. Plus, I'd been with Marcie in too many stores when she'd been followed around by clerks and I could have walked out with a TV in my hands without being even looked at twice. So yeah, I guess he was right.

"We need to get the widest audience possible," Mom added, "because what this company is trying to do is illegal. See?"

She pushed her plate and then the silver pizza tray to the side, and laid out a piece of paper with tiny type. "This is from the Virginia Department of Historic Resources." She slid her finger under one line and read out loud:

Virginia law protects all cemeteries from willful and malicious damage, whether by   the owner   or   by others.

"So clearly showing up near dark with a bulldozer constitutes both willful and malicious damage." She looked up at Isaiah.

"Maybe we need a lawyer," he suggested.

"I was thinking the same thing. But look at this:"

Should you decide to remove and relocate the graves so that the area may be used for other purposes, you are required to file a bill in equity with the city or county circuit court for permission to do so (§57-38.1). This petition will require a good faith effort to identify and contact the families or descendants of the persons interred in the cemetery, as well as publication of a notice of intent in a local newspaper. (§18.2-127).

"Maybe we can find the families of the people buried there?"

I groaned as I took a sip of my root beer. "Shamila already mentioned that. She said it's really hard to find descendants of slaves." Mom looked disappointed. "But she did say she'd be happy to try."

"Alright, then, that's our next step." Isaiah folded his napkin and dropped it on his empty plate. "First, we do a press conference, and then we look for the families of the people buried there."

"And we get a lawyer," Mom added as she stood up to pay the bill, which Isaiah quickly grabbed out of her hands.

"I'll be getting that, thanks." He smiled up at her, and I thought I saw that little spark pass between them. I shook my head and moved toward the door.

The next day, as Mom, Isaiah, and I discussed, I spent every spare minute between classes and at lunch recruiting for the press conference, which would be at 3:30 that afternoon at the cemetery. Mom had called the principal at home last night and, after telling Dr. McMahon what was happening, gotten permission for us to be on school property. Shamila had confirmed with her friend Beatrice, and they would both be there with a camera crew to get the story on the five, six, and eleven o'clock news cycles.

But it wouldn't do to have all this news coverage and only three of us standing there. We had to look like a force, and so I was talking it up with everyone I knew. "Hey, you free this afternoon after school? Want to come be on TV and help save an old slave cemetery?"

After a few times when that line was followed by some strange glances and people traveling quickly through the nearest classroom door, I tried a new tactic. "So this afternoon, a bunch of people are getting together in this old cemetery up on the hill. It's kind of spooky and weird." It was just two weeks before Halloween. "And there's going to be a

TV crew there to talk about it, too. Want to come?"
THAT seemed much more effective.

Marcie helped spread the word, too, and
even got Coach Thomas to let the team out of the
practice for the afternoon so they could come. At
lunch, she and I convinced the whole table to join
us—and when Nicole agreed to skip one dance
practice to be there, I thought Marcie's cheeks
might explode from smiling. Of course, I was
probably no better when Javier said he'd be there,
too. But then when he offered to give me a ride,
well, only the grace of God kept me from snorting
chocolate milk out of my nose.

Before I headed into biology after lunch, I
texted Mom: "We're all set. Lots of folks coming.
Oh, and I don't need you to pick me up. Javier's
giving me a ride."

Now, a lesser parent might have objected,
pointed out the dangers of riding in a car with a
teenage boy, etc., but my mom just wrote back with
twenty smiley emoticons. And I couldn't help but
smile, too.

As soon as the last bell rang, I zipped out
the door and down the steps to the junior/senior
parking lot. I didn't drive myself, just wasn't interested in learning how, but because our school was
the only one in the county and people had to travel

so far to get there, most of the juniors and seniors drove, especially if they played sports.

But Javier wasn't an athlete. He liked music, played drums, in fact, for the jazz band and for his own band—The Screaming Lizards. I'd heard them play once, and they weren't bad if you liked sort of hardcore rock, which I didn't really. I was more into folk stuff. Mom said I was sixteen going on forty.

I waited at the bottom of the concrete stairs until I saw Javier's old beat-up Nissan come from the last row in the lot, and when he pulled up, I opened the door and tried to sound smooth, "Going my way?" (Geez, maybe I *am* forty?)

He smiled and winked. "Get in." Then we zoomed out of the parking lot.

It really might have been possible to walk to the cemetery. It was, after all, just behind the school. But the land was still pretty grown up, and there was a wide patch of trees we'd have to pass through. So driving was easier.

Plus, I was riding with Javier.

I needed to focus.

Earlier that morning, Mom and I had stopped at the cemetery. As soon as I stepped foot on the ground, I saw Moses and waved. Mom saw me and looked where I was looking. It was clear she couldn't see him, but still, she introduced herself. "I'm Elaine Steele, Mary's mom. It's nice to meet you, Moses."

Moses took off his hat and said, "Nice to meet you, too, Miss Steele." I relayed what he'd said to Mom, and then, I walked over so I could explain what was going to be happening that afternoon.

As I talked, we strolled among the fieldstones that marked the graves of people he had known. So many times over the past few days, I had wondered what it must feel like to be the only person you know on the earth and why Moses was still here when none of the other slaves were. I wondered what it must feel like to see their graves every day, to watch cars drive by and know they have no idea about your existence. I imagined Moses was very lonely.

I didn't know how to change that.

But I did know that I had to do all I could to save this cemetery. So after I explained what was happening that afternoon, I asked Moses to tell me about the other people in the cemetery. I couldn't, of course, share that information with anyone because I wouldn't be able to explain how I knew it, but I still thought it might be useful for me to imagine real people with real names when I was talking about the gravesites later today.

"Well, Mary, this here was Monday. She worked out in the fields. She had long, long fingers, and that made her fast with picking—both corn and the banjo. Ooh, whee, that woman could play."

"Nice to meet you, Monday." I said and put my fingers gently on the top of her stone.

"And this was Jesse. He tended the master's garden. Grew the best cabbage you ever ate. Mean as a snake but that cabbage kind of made up for it."

We walked to every stone, and Moses told me about every single person buried there—twenty-three by my count. About Lucy, the young girl who was the nurse for the master's children, who died tragically when she tried to get a doll that the young master's daughter had dropped down a well. About Mildred, the cook who was the only person who could tell the master that he might want to reconsider and who had cheeks as round as a ball. About Scipio, the best preacher on the plantation—"The man could make you feel guilty for not shining up your shoes, Mary." And on and on we went. I wasn't sure if the remembering was helping Moses or just causing him to ache, but he didn't hesitate so I didn't interrupt.

At one particular stone, he paused a long time before he spoke. Finally, he cleared his throat and said only, "This is my wife, Elizabeth."

Then, he pointed to a row of stones beside hers. "Them's my children."

I stared at those five stones, just rocks gathered from the field really, and realized for a first time that people with faces and hobbies and birthmarks and scars lay there. The thought rested like a soft boulder in my chest.

"Thank you, Moses." I didn't really know what to say. His whole family lay there in the ground. I touched my hand to his shoulder blade and felt him shift back against it just a fraction.

I didn't really want to leave Moses there with all those memories freshly brought up, but I heard Mom beep. I smiled at him, but he was still gazing at Elizabeth's stone.

So when Javier and I reached the cemetery, the first thing I did was look for Moses and ask him how his day was, using my cellphone as cover so people wouldn't wonder why I was talking to myself.

"My day was long and short, Mary. Just like all my days. But today, today I spent some time remembering, and that was a good thing."

He pointed to the gravesites around us, and I saw that somehow he had managed to lay a brightly colored leaf from the nearby sugar maple on each grave. A memorial, a sign that they are not forgotten.

On his family's plots, he had tipped three leaves into place, the red of their lives painted into nature.

When Shamila arrived with her friend Beatrice, I asked her to please film those leaves so that they would be a part of the story. Moses smiled.

7

By 3:20, the road was lined with cars. Mom had thought ahead to let VDOT know what was going on, and they'd brought up one of those flashing "event ahead" signs so that people would know to slow down.

I saw a lot of kids from school—my friends, including Marcie and Nicole—but also some other folks like Javier's sister and the girls from the school step team. Word must have gotten out pretty well.

Mom strolled over to me at about 3:25. "You ready?"

I cleared my throat and took a deep breath. I had never given a speech before, let alone on camera. "I guess so."

"Okay, you're going to do great. Mr. Meade is here, and he's so proud of you. Also, just so you don't get distracted when you're talking, the mayor has come, too. I think Shamila might have called him."

"The mayor! Oh, good grief." I took another deep breath. I guess that was a good thing, but like I really needed that pressure.

At 3:30, Isaiah began his introduction. "Ladies and Gentlemen, thank you all for coming. As you know, we are here because we understand that a vital piece of our town's history may be destroyed if we don't take action. We hope that after you hear Ms. Steele's tale, you will decide to join with us to preserve this sacred space. Mary?"

When Isaiah turned to me, somehow, I moved my feet forward and stood in front of the microphone that Beatrice had placed a few minutes earlier. I tried my best to smile, but I expect I looked like one of those pageant girls who smiles with her teeth but shows fear in her eyes. Still, I smiled, took yet another deep breath, and began.

"Ladies and Gentlemen, five nights ago, I was here in this cemetery at about 7:00 o'clock. I'd come for a walk and had stopped to wander amongst these stones that I had just discovered a week ago today." Mom, Isaiah, and I had decided on this story because it was close to the truth but got rid of the pesky issue of me simply appearing in a graveyard. "I find this place to be serene and peaceful. It's a resting place, after all."

I looked over at Moses, who stood just on the edge of the crowd, and he smiled and nodded. "That night, when I was sitting quietly here in this place, a large bulldozer came up the road and, had I not been here, would have pushed over all of these gravestones. In fact, I had to sit on the ground in front of the stones to stop that from happening. My presence as a witness was not enough."

The gasps and cries from the crowd told me that I had made my point, so I forged ahead. "We are not sure, at this time, who was trying to destroy this sacred ground, but we,"—I gestured toward Mom, Isaiah, and Marcie, clustered together to my right—"are determined to find out. What we do know is this— this is a slave burial ground. The people who were enslaved on the Sutton Plantation are buried here beneath these stones." We had set up the press conference just outside the area marked by stones—out of respect—but we were close enough for people to see the fieldstones that marked, Shamila told me, the head and foot of each grave.

"At least twenty-five people were enslaved on this very land until Emancipation freed them. When they died, they were buried here, at the edge of the Sutton Plantation. Their graves have gone unnoted on maps and records for two hundred years, but now, we are giving notice. This place is hallowed ground, and we will *not* let it be disturbed."

The crowd cheered, and I was surprised at the level of emotion in my own voice. I had been shouting, and I was near tears. I looked again at Moses, and he dipped his chin with encouragement.

"We are working with the Malhalland Historical Society to save this place, and we need your help. First, we need people to agree to come and help us clean the cemetery of fallen limbs and debris." We had set out these steps last night, various ways for people to get involved that required several levels of commitment and skill. "Shamila Jones from the Historical Society will be leading up that effort. She will also be coordinating volunteers who would like to do research on the Sutton Plantation, and particularly, on the people who were enslaved there."

I took a deep breath here because this was the hard request, the dangerous one. "Finally, we need people to help us figure out who is trying to destroy these graves. While most people—including school officials—had no idea these graves were on school land, someone did, and that someone sought to destroy them. We need to know who that person is."

People exchanged anxious glances, but a few heads nodded as I continued. "The school board has agreed to designate the cemetery and a ten-foot buffer on all sides as a sacred space. As part of our community service requirement, students will be coming here to erect a split rail fence around the property, and the art department is already at work on a fitting sign and monument to these individuals."

"But all of that will be useless if we don't keep this land protected. " Mom had asked the school to have a security guard patrol this part of the property for the past few nights. There had been no sign of heavy machinery, but we figured it was only a matter of time. We couldn't guard it forever. "The best way for us to do that is to spread the word that this place is off-limits, so please go home and tell your families. Share the news with your colleagues and churches. And stop by the table near the road,"—Marcie had moved over by the table,"—to pick up 'Save the Sutton Slave Cemetery' fliers to hang around town. Finally, if you'd like to help with clean-up or research, or have any news to share about who might want to destroy this cemetery, please stop by and talk to me, my mom, or Isaiah Perkins. " They both waved. "We will keep your name and information in the strictest confidence, and you will know you have done good work."

On a whim, I deviated from the script: "Who's with me? Who wants to save the Sutton Slave Cemetery?" A cheer rang out across the mountains, and if I wasn't mistaken, I saw tears at the edges of Moses's eyes.

By the time we left the cemetery, the sun had hidden itself away behind the ridge, and we had over fifty people signed up to help with the objectives we set out, including two local genealogists who would help Shamila research the Sutton plantation and the enslaved people who lived, worked, and died there. While I answered questions that Beatrice would cut into the feed of the press conference on the news tonight, I noticed that Isaiah was talking to two men a little distance away from the rest of the crowd. When he saw me watching him, he gave me a tiny, brisk nod. Maybe they knew something about who had come to try and dig up these graves.

As the last of the cars pulled off from the side of the road, Mom, Isaiah, Marcie, Nicole, Javier, Shamila, and I gathered near Mom's car, tossing the few remaining fliers and the folded, plastic table into her back seat. "Well, I'd say that was a success," Mom began.

"Me, too," Shamila said. "I've been doing history in this town for a long time, and that's the most excited I've seen anyone about anything old besides when they changed the road name over on Ford's Gap."

I just remembered that controversy. When they put in the new 911 system that required all the roads to be named, not just labeled with state route numbers, people got upset because Ford's Gap Road, which had really been two roads that intersected with one another near Bentley Ford's old store, had been renamed. The bigger road kept the name, but the smaller one had gotten named "Ford Store Road" so that emergency responders wouldn't get confused by the addresses.

"Agreed," Isaiah spoke quietly. "But there weren't many African American people here today." He looked at Marcie, then Beatrice, then Shamila before looking to me, and then Mom. "We'll need them to make this work. After all, it's most likely that the descendants of the people buried here are black, and so we'll need their request to prevent any future digging."

"So how do we get more African Americans to come out?" Mom asked.

"Beatrice said that she can prepare tonight's news story so that it's clear we want African American involvement, and then, maybe we can call on some of the pastors from black churches around. Let them know what's happening so they can tell their congregations," Isaiah said.

"Mom did talk to the deacons at our church, so I'll ask if we can follow up with an announcement at church on Sunday," Marcie said.

"Great. Thanks. Meanwhile, I'll keep working to find out who the people buried here might have been, and as I get leads, I'll ask those two genealogists to trace their family lines. When we find kin here in Terra Linda, folks will get even more interested."

"Mary, maybe you and I can get some of the students involved, too." Mr. Meade had been on the phone over by his car when we started this impromptu meeting and had joined us in the midst of our conversation. "You guys can get community service credit for helping Shamila with research and working on the graveyard itself. Would that help?" He looked at Isaiah.

"Yeah, that would be great. The more parts of our community—all parts of our community—who are involved, the more power we'll have. And I think we may need all the power we can get."

All of us followed the line of his gaze to see a group of four or five white men standing by a grove of trees on the other side of the cemetery. They had been here for the whole press conference and stood talking quietly and looking at us every once in a while.

"That's it. I'm going over there." Mom started to march that way when Isaiah put a gentle hand on her arm. "Ellen, wait. Let's not antagonize them. They'll come to us when they're ready."

We didn't have to wait long.   When I checked my Facebook wall just before going to sleep last night, I had dozens of posts and messages, almost all of them from friends congratulating us on the news story and asking how they could be involved.

But one message was different. Someone named Layoff Steele had written, "Stop now, Miss Steele, before you regret ever 'taking a walk' in that cemetery."

8

When I came down for breakfast the next morning, I wondered if Mom had slept at all. She had her phone clamped to her ear and papers scattered all over the kitchen table. But ever vigilant, she had also made me a plate of scrambled eggs with cheese and thick-cut maple bacon. As Mom talked—"No, I'm not overly concerned . . . just wanted you to be aware..."—she even poured me a cup of coffee. Coffee was a rare treat for me, something Mom reserved only for those days when she thought I might need a little more than average fortification.

When she hung up, she sat down and wrapped her hands around her own mug. "How did you sleep?"

"Okay. Thanks. *Did* you sleep?"

"Of course. I just got up early to take care of a few things. Speaking of which, Javier will be here in about fifteen minutes to pick you up for school."

I nearly spit bacon at her, which would have been a serious waste. One does not spit out bacon. "What?! You called Javier! *Mom!!*"

"I didn't want you riding the bus to school, and I can't take you today. Isaiah and I have a meeting with two pastors at 8:30 this morning. Besides, I thought you'd like the chance to ride with Javier."

Quickly, I flashed all those '80s movies with teenage girls getting ready for dates—piles of clothes and shoes tossed willy-nilly on the bed, hours of make-up prep—and sighed. I was not one of those girls. Instead, I tugged my clawed fingers through my curls, pulled half my hair in a make-shift bun at the back of my head, and checked to be sure I hadn't worn this shirt in the last week. All clear. I was good to go.

And Mom was right. I was a little excited.

"I've also called the school to let them know you've received a threat."

I didn't like that idea either, but I figured she was probably wise. The message had been sent from a fake Facebook account that led to a brand-new Gmail address, so I had no idea who sent it. But it had scared me, so while I was a bit mortified by Mom's actions, I was also grateful.

"I'll be there to pick you up, and we'll go over to the Historical Society. Mr. Meade is coming, too, because he wants to see what specific assignments he can create for class and get some ideas of research avenues."

I tossed the last bite of bacon into my mouth. "Thanks, Mom," I mumbled just as I heard the beep of Javier's car. I gave her a quick kiss on the cheek, threw my backpack over my right shoulder, and walked out the front door. Today was going to be quite the day.

The ride in was uneventful if you don't count the fact that at first I could barely speak and then overcompensated by rambling on about ghosts and what people say they are and why they are in certain places for the full fifteen-minute ride. *Way to go, Mary. Freak him out with not only ghost stuff but freaky science stuff, too.*

When I eventually took a breath, Javier said, "I believe in ghosts. My grandmother sees them all the time."

I must have looked puzzled because he continued, "Well, not *all* the time. Like not at the grocery store and stuff. But in old houses and near cemeteries."

"How does she know they're ghosts? I mean, couldn't she just be seeing things? I mean, isn't she kind of old?" As soon as I spoke, I could have opened the car door and rolled out onto the pavement. *Isn't she kind of old?   Really, Mary, have you no tact, no filter at all?*

Javier just laughed. "I guess. She's sixty-two. She's seen them all her life, ever since she was a little girl."

"Wow. That's kind of cool." I took a deep breath. "Do you ever see ghosts?"

"Nah, Granny says I don't have that kind of sight. That my gift is more for machines than people."

Granny apparently hadn't met me and my big mouth yet.

"What about you?" he asked.

Two weeks ago, I would have just said, "Nope. I think people do, but I haven't. Might be cool though." But today, today was very different. I almost whispered, "I've seen one."

"You have? Cool. Where?" Javier barely took his eyes off the road to glance at me. Clearly, this was not a huge deal for him.

I wasn't sure though. I really liked this guy, and even if he didn't feel the same way about me, I didn't want him thinking I was nuts. And if he was interested, I didn't want to scare him off. Plus, I didn't think he was the rumor-starting type, but I wasn't sure. What if he told his grandmother, and she scoffed because she knew I didn't have that kind of sight either. A girl can do a lot of panicking in the course of thirty seconds.

I finally settled on a phrase I've heard Mom say dozens of times: "The truth will set you free, even if it hurts. "

"Well, I see a ghost in the slave cemetery at the Sutton Place."

Javier gave the wheel a little twist, but he recovered quickly. "You do? Who is it?"

"His name is Moses, and he was a slave."

"Whoa, you know his name? That's incredible. How did you figure it out? "

"He told me."

This time, Javier pulled the car off the road. "He told you? Granny says ghosts don't speak. How did he tell you? Did he write it down or something, or did you actually hear him?" He was staring at me with this intensity that made my heart lurch.

"No, I just hear him like I'm hearing you now. " I thought about telling Javier that Isaiah could do the same thing, but then, that wasn't really my secret to tell. "I talk to him every time I go to the cemetery. He's always there."

Javier looked back across the steering wheel, and I felt that rise of panic again. *Too much, I'd said too much.*

Then, he leaned over and kissed me, quick and gentle, right on the lips, before pulling the car back on the road and finishing the drive.

Apparently, having a freakish ability was a turn-on.   I didn't need spectral feet to float into the building.

It didn't take me long to come back to earth though. Javier walked me to my homeroom and gave me this killer smile as he walked away—"See you at lunch,"—and I felt a little swimmy-headed as I made it to my seat. But before I sat down, I was surrounded by people who had questions, who wanted to volunteer, who thought it was weird that I wanted to work in a slave graveyard. I had never been so grateful for the late bell.

Fortunately, Marcie and I have our first two classes together, so she helped me field questions, take down names, and shoot witty retorts to the "cool" kids who made comments about "grave-diggers" and "history freaks." The comments didn't really bother me. When you've been the smart kid all your life in a small town, you get used to it. But it did feel good to have those smartasses taken down a peg by the school's star athlete.

Between classes and questions, I managed to tell Marcie about Javier's kiss, and she grinned. "I figured something had happened. You're kind of glowing."

"And what about Nicole? Anything happening there?"

"Maybe. She and I are going to hang fliers about the cemetery together after school today. I'll keep you posted."

Now, it was my turn to smile.

The period just before lunch was Mr. Meade's history class, and so I was actually looking forward to that one. I sat in my usual spot—second column, third seat back—and took out my navy blue binder that was full of my history notes. I had just opened to a new page, when I felt a hand grip my shoulder. I looked up to see a big snub-nosed, white kid glaring down at me.

I knew him, had known him since we were three—Blanchard Perry. Everyone called him Blanch. He was pretty quiet and hung out with a couple other guys who seemed to enjoy fishing and hunting—they were always out of school on the first day of hunting season. School wasn't Blanch's favorite, a fact he made very obvious by sitting in the back of every class and looking as bored as possible. But he wasn't a bad guy, at least I hadn't thought so. But this expression scared me a little.

"What's up, Blanch?"

"Mary, I'm here to give you a warning. Some people really don't like what you're doing up at that cemetery. I mean, they *really* don't like it."

I would never have pegged Blanch for the threatening type. But here he was, a huge hand squeezing my shoulder and a look of utter contempt on his face.

He continued. "So watch yourself."

I must have looked scared because he quickly took back his hand. "Sorry. I mean, I just want you to be careful. I've heard some things that my dad and his friends are talking about, and well, they're really angry. I don't understand it, but I think you could get into some danger if you aren't careful. I just wanted to warn you and let you know that I've got your back." He turned a little pink when he said those last words.

Oh my goodness, Blanchard Perry was offering to be my bodyguard. The hilarity of that offer was so vast that I almost laughed out loud. That Blanch would want to protect me was funny in and of itself, but that I would need protection—that would have been hysterical if it wasn't terrifying.

I looked up at Blanch. "Thanks so much. I really appreciate both the heads up and the lookout. That's really sweet of you."

Now he was full-on blushing, a red sweeping up from his neck to the top of his nose. "It's nothing. Just you and me have been friends a long time, and I know you're a good person."

"Thanks, Blanch." I laid my hand over his and gave it a squeeze. I thought the boy's head might explode from too much blood flow and quickly pulled my hand away. If I didn't know better, I'd say Blanch Perry had a crush on me.

Just then, the bell rang and Blanch moseyed back to his seat, the color slowly receding from his ears.

I couldn't help but smile. It kind of felt good to have a bodyguard.

A few minutes later, I forgot all about Blanch's kindness. Mr. Meade was introducing the class cemetery project, and I was studying all the faces in the room, trying to gauge if people were excited or bored.

To my relief, people were actually looking interested. Some were taking notes; others were just listening. Only a couple folks were tuned out completely, the air outside the windows apparently much more fascinating.

The project would work like this: students would divide into four groups; one to research the Sutton family; one to research the plantations and farms around the Sutton place; one to research the history of slavery in Malhalland County; and one to work with Shamila and her volunteers on the gene-alogy of the people enslaved on the Sutton planta-tion.

We would be using the records at the His-torical Society and the County Clerk's office—Shamila was doing a training for everyone on Fri-day afternoon—as well as interviewing local people and looking at church records in the area. The pro-ject was going to take the rest of the year, with our mid-term focused on research methods and the final a presentation by each group on their findings.

Mr. Meade didn't mention this, but I knew he'd had to pull some pretty hefty strings to make this happen because it didn't follow the SOL guidelines (our aptly-named state standardized tests). But had he assured the principal and the school board that his students would ace those tests?

Today, all he said was that he would be holding special study sessions for the SOLs for anyone who wanted to attend and he would be making a list of historically-accurate films that we could watch in preparation. The class clapped for that suggestion.

It didn't take long for us to divide ourselves up, but I was surprised at who ended up in what group. Some of the more popular girls in class really wanted to do the farm research because they were interested in learning about their own family history, and some of the really quiet guys—including Blanch—jumped at the chance to do some genealogical research. (It did not, however, escape my attention that Blanch waited to see that I had joined the genealogical group before sauntering over.)

Things didn't break out on racial lines either. A fair number of black kids wanted to look into the Suttons and the other plantations as well as the history of slavery, and a bunch of white kids went immediately to the slavery group. I took some encouragement there, and Mr. Meade did, too.

"I'm so glad to see that you guys have picked areas that interest you, and I'm so glad to see that all of you recognize that the history of slavery and the stories of enslaved people are the history and story of America—*all* of America." I saw a few heads nodding at his pronouncement.

We used the rest of the class period to begin planning our research. Mr. Meade was going to give us half of every period for this project—using the other half to give short lectures on the various other subjects in US History—and we would have every Friday's period to share our week's findings and talk about our next steps. Our group on gene-alogy talked about getting an Ancestry.com sub-scription—something Shamila had suggested—and I told them we could use my mom's account; I was sure she wouldn't mind. We also figured we should see if we knew anyone who had ancestors who lived up that way and decided we'd all ask our friends—both black and white—if they were related to the Suttons. We didn't have any Suttons at school, but maybe someone's grandma was a Sut-ton.

By the time the bell rang, we had agreed that tomorrow we'd come back to share whatever we had found, and I knew I had to figure out a way to share Moses's story without talking about ghosts.

But first, Javier . . . I mean, lunch. I took my seat with my standard tray of pizza, chocolate milk, and Oreos—if my mother knew, I'd be packing every day. Before long Marcie dropped down across from me with Nicole at her side. Our other friends, Susan and Daequan, sat down, too, and then I felt a hand skim my back as Javier sat down right next to me. Marcie opened her eyes really wide and smiled. I'm sure I was blushing worse than Blanch.

Javier's lunch would make my mom proud—salad, cottage cheese, fresh fruit. I supposed other girls would be embarrassed by this plate of junk I had in front of me, especially when the guy they liked was eating such healthy food, but I was famished and didn't really have time to be ashamed as I shoved that pizza into my face. Besides, it was best that Javier really know what he was getting into.

We talked for a while about school stuff—the two girls who had gotten in a fight and pulled each other's hair out, Marcie's upcoming tournament over in Harrisonburg, the crazy fact that we were soon going to dissect baby pigs. (I had been working on how to get out of biology for that week for about a month now.)

Just then, a girl—her name was Tina, I thought—stomped over to our table. "You. You need to mind your own business."

At first, I thought she was talking to someone behind me. But when I felt Javier sit up straighter and saw Marcie plant both her feet on the floor as if she as going to stand up, I realized this girl was talking to me. People didn't normally speak to me that way, you know, mean and all. "I'm sorry. I don't know what you're talking about."

"Yes, you do. Don't play dumb. I saw you on TV. You need to stop messing around with all this cemetery stuff." By now, a small group of kids had gathered behind her—a couple of guys and two other girls, all people I'd known my whole life but didn't really know well. "You're screwing around with things you don't know anything about. So back off."

It probably speaks to my love of mystery novels that my first response to this statement was *Ah, similar language to the Facebook threat last night* and not either fear or anger. But really, I was mostly puzzled. "Why? Why should I back off?"

At this point, I saw Blanch move in behind me, and I must have kind of smiled as Javier took my hand under the table because the girl lunged, tossing my tray past my face and leaning in really close. She had great skin.

"Because you might get hurt."

Clearly, I was insane because my next statement was "No, I realize that. What I mean is why is what I'm doing so threatening to someone? I mean, we're just trying to save a cemetery. Why would people care enough about that to make threats?"

I realized my mistake just as I felt Javier tug me toward him and watched Blanch's large hand reach over my head to grab the girl's speeding fist. Jeez, I guess I did need a bodyguard after all.

Just then, the teacher on lunch duty caught sight of the situation and came over to investigate. Tina backed off and walked to her table, and Blanch took a seat next to Javier.   As I finally realized that I had just about been punched, I felt tears stinging my eyes. Marcie looked at me, "Mary Louise Steele, you are either the bravest or the stupidest person I know."

I smiled as a tear slipped down my cheek.

9

The next few weeks whizzed by. Between class, research, Thanksgiving, and dates with Javier, I almost didn't realize it was time for mid-terms and Christmas. The tests were not a concern for me. Like I've said, I was good at school. My trouble was making sure I did well on the tests without looking like I did *that* well. This skill required a lot of pencil chewing, staring off into space, and repeated flipping back-throughs of my completed exam. I still almost always finished first, but at least I hoped it didn't seem like I was showing off.

What I was worried about was our presentation for Mr. Meade's class. Our group had done a lot of research—launched by Shamila's wise choice to share Moses's identity as a kind of oral tradition, thus getting us started without outing me as a ghost seer. Shamila told us a story about Moses and his wife, Elizabeth, and suggested we take a look at the 1870 census.

When I saw "Elizabeth Perkins" in the list of people in Malhalland County, it took everything I had to not sprint up the hill to tell Moses, but of course, that was out of the question; both because it would have seemed strange, and because I can't run around the block without being chased, much less two miles up a hill. So I had to wait until my way home.

Javier had taken to driving me to and from school and research gatherings—he'd become an impromptu member of our research team—and on this day, I kissed him quickly as he dropped me off at the cemetery at my request. I told him I just wanted to spend some time there, which wasn't unusual since I usually asked to be let out there at least once a week. It seemed important to me that I get to know the place and the people we were try-ing to find. Plus, I really liked Moses.

As soon as Javier's car pulled away, Moses walked over, and something about my expression must have given me away because he said, "What is it, Miss Mary? Did you find something?"

Moses knew all about our research. I'd done my best to keep him posted. While he wasn't thrilled with us digging into things that could get us in trouble, he was excited by what we were find-ing. I gave him a report every week, and he con-firmed or challenged what we found. For example, he definitely agreed that the Sutton family—Maurice and Amanda—had five children, including Millie, who caught tuberculosis and died when she was six.

But Moses didn't agree with some other things. He told me that the slave traders didn't re-ally come through these parts, like the slavery re-search team thought. There just weren't enough slaves in the mountains, so if someone wanted to sell or buy a slave, they went east to Richmond. Shamila and I quickly figured out a way to correct my classmates's interpretation by sharing a book about the Richmond slave auction.

Whether he knew it or not, Moses was the heart of our research team, and today, I was so ea-ger to tell him I'd seen his family's names. I'd even made a copy of the census to show him.

But he didn't react like I thought he would. I had expected joy, maybe tinged with sadness. I didn't ever imagine that he'd rip the paper to shreds.

"Moses! What in the world?!"

He stood with his back to me, and his hands were shaking. After a few moments, he faced me and said, "I'm sorry, Miss Mary. I shouldn't have ripped up your paper."

"Oh goodness, don't worry about that. We can always get another copy." But the look on his face told me he didn't ever want to see that list again.

"What is wrong, Moses?" I laid my hand on his arm.

He stared at my fingers for a long time. "Elijah, Mary, though I loved him something fierce, Elijah weren't mine."

I looked at the shreds of white now floating through the crisp air like snow. What did he mean? The census listed him as Elizabeth's son; I was confused. I stared up into Moses's face.

"Elijah was the master's son, Mary. Master Maurice's and Elizabeth's boy."

I didn't know what to say. So I just squeezed Moses's arm a little tighter and stared across the mountainside with him.

When I got back to the Historical Society the next afternoon, Shamila was ready with lots of information for me. The rest of the team was still at school, plowing through Ancestry.com records to fill in the family tree now that we had more names to follow, but I wanted to talk with Shamila about what Moses had told me. I'd sent her an email the night before, and she'd replied, "I was afraid we might find this. Come see me tomorrow."

So here I was, confused, upset, angry, even. What did it mean that Moses's son was not his own? How was that possible? I knew something was not right, but exactly what that was, I couldn't say.

"Mary, sit down." Shamila and I dropped into the wing chairs by the front windows in the sitting room of the house. "As a woman, I know you are already aware of how you have to watch out for certain things. You know, to take care of yourself in ways that Javier and other boys don't have to. You don't go into dark places by yourself. You don't leave yourself alone in a room with a boy you don't know. Right?"

I nodded. Of course, I knew these things. Every girl I was friends with realized that while it was ridiculous that we had to be fearful this way and that it really shouldn't have to be our responsibility to keep men from attacking us, we couldn't count on that. "Sure."

"Okay, so imagine you are an enslaved woman. You have no choice about where you go and when. You can only travel, sleep, relax when your master or mistress let you. Then, imagine that your master owns you, thinks of you as a piece of property that is like anything else in his possession—a chair perhaps—but a desirable chair. One that can give him pleasure and reinforce his power."

I wasn't that naive. I knew about rape, and I could see that enslaved women must have been in special danger of it. "Right. Elizabeth was probably raped. I understand." I wasn't trying to be flippant, but Shamila seemed to be giving more weight to this than I comprehended.

"Right, Mary. Elizabeth was raped. And that alone would be horrible. Absolutely horrible. But I don't think you understand. Elizabeth was probably raped over and over again for years. She might have simply had to accept this horror as part of her life, something she couldn't change if she wanted to be safe and keep her family safe, too. In many situations, slave masters had favorite women who they used for just this purpose at their whim and will. It's quite possible that it wasn't just Elijah that wasn't Moses's son. It might have been that none of his children were his own."

I sat in that wing chair for a long time, Shamila filing and making notes around me. "Raped over and over again." I kept playing those words against the curves of my brain, but no matter how much I tried I just couldn't imagine it. I couldn't picture how any woman could let that happen to her. *I would have run*, I thought. But then I would have to leave my family and friends, and I might be in even more danger, if that was possible. *I would have killed the man.* But then I'd be killed. The harder I thought the more a shadow of desperation sank over me. I couldn't help Elizabeth, even in my imagination. The nightmare of her days, knowing that this man could come for her whenever he felt like it.

I sat long into the evening, silent sobs racking my chest.

Over the next few days, with a little more research and a very hard conversation with Moses, we learned that he had four children: Elijah, Claudia, Minerva, and Tom; only Claudia was his biological child, or at least he thought she was his child. Her skin was darker than her brothers and sisters', so he thought maybe she was his. But he couldn't know. He would never know.

He was certain, though, that Elijah, Minerva, and Tom were not his children. Their skin was lighter—so that was one indicator—but he also knew that he'd been away in Norfolk with Master Sutton's brother-in-law, Steven, at the times when those babies were made. It wasn't possible that they were his, and he knew Elizabeth—she wasn't taking other men to her bed willingly.

So here, on this morning before the holiday break, I was as nervous as could be when Javier picked me up. The principal had decided she wanted Mr. Meade's class to present our findings as part of the holiday assembly, so we would be talking about our work before the whole school. Tina's threats had slowed down, but she still glowered at me every time I passed. Fortunately, I was almost always with other people - Marcie and Nicole, or Blanch or Javier—so she never tried to hurt me again. Still, I knew she'd be in the audience, and I didn't relish sharing this news since—if I was right—this is part of why someone wanted this cemetery destroyed.

Plus, the idea of talking about this ugly part of slavery, well, it wasn't going to be easy. After Shamila had given me the full picture, after I'd had time to sit with it and imagine what it would have been to live not only as an enslaved person but as a woman who could not even protect herself, whose husband could not protect her . . . my eyes still filled and my chest still hurt at the thought.

Just before lunch, I was on stage, looking at every one I knew. Mom and Isaiah were in the front row with Mr. Meade and Shamila. Beatrice and her cameraman were over to the side. I didn't even know if I could tell the story of Moses's family without crying. I tried to believe what Mom had said to me over breakfast. "It's okay that you cry, Mary. Your tears will just show how important this story is."

The Sutton family researchers went first, sharing what they'd found about Maurice and Amanda, their children, and the plantation itself. Then, the farm research group talked about other farms in the area, wisely focusing on the farm families who had descendants in the room. People were definitely interested to hear about their ancestors.

Then, the slavery research team talked. They described the unique experience of slavery in the Virginia mountains, how most plantations had only a few slaves and, thus, the Sutton plantation was rare in this area because so many people were enslaved there. They talked about the law that prevented the education of slaves in the state and how slaves were not allowed to legally marry but that many still lived—if they were permitted—as family units. They showed images of the Richmond slave auction and put up copies of runaway slave ads. Then, they talked about the most violent parts of the system—whippings, sales, and rapes.

The audience was very quiet—some people were crying—when I began to talk.

I began by telling the story of Moses Perkins, the enslaved man who tended the master's horses. I talked about the kind of work he might have done and what he might have looked like. (Of course, I knew what he looked like, but I had to pretend I didn't.) Then, I talked about his wife, Elizabeth, what she did as the seamstress, how she made all the clothes for the enslaved community— rough, quick garments made from unsoftened cotton—and how she also did fine needlework for the mistress's gowns, how her embroidery skills were, I expect, masterful. I even slipped in the possibility that she might have quilted—although Moses said she didn't—because I knew that some of the classes talked about the sketchy legend about quilts used to signal folks on the Underground Railroad.

Then, I shared the facts about Moses's and Elizabeth's children, the way they are listed on the census and even a bit that Shamila had taught me about what their lives would have been like after Emancipation. We also knew that some of their children and grandchildren had ended up living in the North, moving as part of the Great Migration, but I didn't mention that. I didn't want to dilute the impact of the story I really needed to tell. The one I knew would hit hardest.

I glanced quickly at Mom, and she gave me a smile and a nod.

"But none of Moses's children except Claudia—as much as he loved them as such—were his flesh and blood. They were Maurice Sutton's children with Moses's wife, Elizabeth."

I could almost see it flash through their reality-TV shaped minds—Elizabeth had cheated on Moses—but quickly, I changed the screen from the census record I had been showing to an image of a young black woman running from a young white man. It was a sketch done in 1859 for the Abolitionist movement, and it was entitled "Slave Woman Does Not Want More of Her Master's Babies."

I let the image sit for a few seconds, just until I saw a few mouths open with surprise. We all knew about rape. We even knew two girls who had been raped who were in this very room. (Mr. Meade had asked the school nurse to give anyone who might be affected a warning about the content of the talk.) But to think about rape in this context, with the background of slavery and ownership that my classmates had just established, that was different, even if they, like I, had trouble putting just how into words.

"Elizabeth Perkins was raped by her master, Maurice Sutton. She was raped over and over again for many years. We know this because we know—from Sutton's diary and the ages of her children on the census record—that Moses was not on the plantation during the times when three of his children were conceived." Of course, I also knew it because Moses told me it was true. Goodness I wished he could be here to hear this story told out loud. But maybe—probably—he wouldn't have wanted to hear it.

I waited a second, expecting someone, Tina maybe, to shout that she could have been with other enslaved men. It didn't have to be the master. That's what the Internet conversation often came to when the children of masters and slaves came up. It's what people still said about Sally Hemmings and Thomas Jefferson—those children could not be Jefferson's despite all the evidence that said they were.

But the crowd stayed quiet.

At this point, Mr. Meade took over, and I sat down in the row of chairs at the back of the stage with my classmates. I was shaking, and I felt like I could drink an entire gallon of sweet tea, but I had done my part . . . and now, now we moved forward.

Mr. Meade explained that our research in the spring would involve trying to find all the descendants of Moses Perkins and Maurice Sutton, that it was our hope that finding these descendants would not only help to save the Sutton Slave Cemetery but also bring to light some of Terra Linda's hardest but most important history. Then, he thanked everyone for coming, and we filed off the stage as the choir came on to sing a few songs and end the assembly.

I anticipated that I'd get some flack as I left the auditorium, and apparently Javier and Blanch thought the same thing and flanked me like I was Rhianna leaving a restaurant. All they needed were the black suits and the earpieces to complete the look.

But no one said anything to me that day . . . or the next. In fact, we made it all the way through Christmas before the response came, but when it did, it almost toppled us all like gravestones under a bulldozer.

10

My childhood hadn't been really easy; no dad, single mom and all that, but for the most part, people had been kind to me. Sure, kids had been cruel like we were, telling me I couldn't play a particular game or saying mean things about the zits that showed up on my forehead when I was twelve. (Well-meaning adults always tried to tell me that oily skin now meant young skin later, and I always smiled and said, "Thank you." But really I wanted to say, "Do you even remember what it was like to *be* young?") Mostly, people were gracious and supportive of my mom and me. They had us over for holiday meals so we didn't have to be alone. They gave me their best hand-me-downs since they knew that sometimes it was hard for Mom to buy me new clothes. Generally, people were very nice.

So I had grown to believe that the world—while hard—was made up of mostly kind, caring people who would never do or say cruel things to me. While I saw the wounds of such cruelty lived out in Mom's office every day—in the bruised eyes of young women trying to decide if they could leave their husbands and in the young men so battered by the abusive words of their parents that they doubled over and cried every week—Mom always reminded me, when I started to blast the cruel ones, that everyone had a reason for doing what they did. That while we didn't excuse horrible behavior, we also didn't condemn people for it. We tried to understand everyone's pain.

It was a great gift, that lesson. Really, it was, even if I didn't always think so.

I especially didn't think so on the morning two days after Christmas when Mom and I woke up to find our entire yard full of grave-sized holes with gravestones at their heads, every one of them with my name or Mom's name on it.

All that teaching about kindness and compassion didn't prepare me for how to deal with this kind of cruelty. So I fell down in the yard and lay there sobbing until Mom finished calling the police. Then, Marcie, Javier, and Isaiah arrived, and I wandered into the house in the midst of them and dropped to the couch.

As everyone arrived one by one, they joined Mom and me in the living room, picking up mugs of something hot as they came through the kitchen. (Even in her own crisis, Mom showed hospitality.) Isaiah was the first to arrive and came right to us and knelt down—"Are you two okay?"

"Yes, yes, we are. Physically at least. We didn't even know it had happened until this morning," Mom said as I gave her a skeptical look out of the corner of my eye.

Then, Isaiah stood and went to the window to stare. If I had wanted to label his expression, I might call it "resigned anger." Somehow, even through my own tears, I thought maybe Isaiah knew a bit more about this kind of hatefulness than I did.

Javier arrived next with Marcie close behind. He sat down beside me, put his arm around my shoulders, and let me bury my face in his chest. He didn't say a thing, but just held me.

Marcie sat with Mom on the floor by the fireplace and began to talk. Who could have done this? Why? How did they know where we lived? Isaiah soon joined, and the sleuthing pulled me out of my tears.

"At least it didn't happen *on* Christmas," Marcie said.

Mom agreed. "I was thinking the same thing."

"Oh no," Isaiah almost whispered. "They wouldn't have done this on Christmas. Too many people out and about that day. Now everyone is going back to work, so there's less chance of them being seen."

I hadn't even thought of that. I had imagined to think that this was spontaneous, a more intense version of someone deciding to TP someone's house. But if Isaiah was right, this was calculated, deliberately cruel, and planned. I felt the tears sour the back of my eyes again.

"I think we should call Beatrice." I was as surprised as anyone else when Javier spoke. He was usually pretty quiet, involved in what was happening, eager to help, but content to not take the lead. Here, though, this was bold, and I could tell by a glance at everyone's faces that they liked both this boldness and his idea.

Isaiah had Beatrice on the phone within a minute. She'd be over in an hour with a camera crew. She wanted to be sure to film the police on scene as well as interview Mom and me as soon as possible.

Just then, the police arrived. They'd been waylaid by a Christmas tree fire downtown, one of the officers told Mom. They were sorry to keep us.

Even in her distress, Mom just nodded; of course, a fire took precedence over vandalism.

The officers asked Mom and me questions—who might have done this? Did we have any idea why graves and headstones? We reminded them that we were Mary and Elaine Steele, the two women leading the Save The Sutton Cemetery Campaign. Most of the officers nodded, but I noticed one younger man step a bit closer to us, his gaze intent.

When the rest of the uniformed folks moved away, he came over to me. Mom was talking to Isaiah nearby, and I was still shaken. I didn't have much resilience this morning, and something about this man put me on edge even though he looked familiar.

"Mary?"

"Yes." I took a step back from him as he inched even closer.

"I'm Stephen. Tina's brother. Remember? I was a few years ahead of you."

It was my turn to lean in. "Stephen, Stephen Douglas. Right. I remember you."

"Good. Good. So how did you get mixed up in all this mess anyway?"

The fact that he was Tina's brother wasn't putting me at ease, but I did know him—and there were lots of people around. "Well, I just took a walk to the cemetery one day . . . ." I told him the whole story—leaving out Moses, of course—and at moments, he seemed quite surprised.

"So you didn't go trying to find a cause, trying to stir stuff up? This wasn't some publicity stunt to get you a big college scholarship and get your mom more of her shrink clients?" He and I both winced at that phrase for my mom's work. Clearly, his opinion of therapists was not high, but he did look a bit chagrinned at his own prejudice.

"Nope, totally fell into it. But I'm glad I did. If I hadn't been there that night, the bulldozer would have taken out all those graves, and no one would have even known people were buried there."

Stephen was staring at some imaginary something over my right shoulder. "That's very interesting. Not what I had heard at all."

I wasn't sure he had intended to say that out loud, but I wasn't going to let that go.

"What do you mean?"

His eyes snapped back to me. "Oh, just that the story I was told was that this was some sort of publicity stunt, something you drummed up for your own purposes. I should have known better than to believe him."

"Who?"

He paused just a moment and looked me in the eye. "My dad. Well, my dad and his friends."

"What does your dad have to do with this?"

He looked a bit sheepish again. "Oh, he was the man driving the bulldozer that night, Mary." He looked around quickly. "It's his construction firm that's trying to get the bid for the ball fields, and they needed to get rid of the graveyard in order to be able to put in the lowest bid. But you didn't hear that from me."

So we had been right. It was about the construction. "You're a police officer! Why didn't you tell anyone?"

"Honestly, I should have, but I wasn't really sure until I came here today. That handwriting there, that's my sister's. I'd recognize it anywhere." He pointed to a big headstone with my name practically carved into the Styrofoam with a large, black marker. The handwriting was curly and bubbly, definitely a girl's writing. "See that smiley face over the i in 'died,'" I did, right next to the year 2014, "that's Tina's signature thing. She's been doing that since she was little."

Stephen's words took my breath. Despite Tina's threats at lunch that day and her continued chilly disposition, I hadn't imagined she could be this cruel. But then, people did many things to protect their families. I would.

See, always look for the *why* behind someone's actions, and you can find a way to compassion. Still, compassion or not, I was pissed.

"What are you going to do?" I whirled back around to Stephen. He was making notes in that little spiral notebook that was apparently part of the policeman's official get-up, not just a *Law and Order* prop.

"I think, Mary, that probably we should all talk." He pointed to Mom and Isaiah, and to Javier and Marcie. "I think you will all want to hear this."

Just then, Beatrice pulled up with the news van. "Damn it. Who called the news?" another police officer shouted.

"We did." Mom walked over to meet Beatrice as she climbed out of the van. They hugged, and Beatrice directed her cameraman to film everything—stones, graves, and the police officers. Then, Beatrice came over.

I glanced at Stephen, and he gave me a quick nod. "Beatrice, I think you'll also want to talk with Stephen Douglas. He apparently knows something about not only this"—I swung my arm out over the yard—"but about the cemetery, too."

Mom gave me a puzzled look but directed us all into the house, where she quickly put on more coffee and hot water for tea. This day was going to require a lot of warm mugs, it seemed.

By the time Stephen finished telling us what he knew about the events of the past few months, I felt like someone had pulled my lungs out of my mouth, twisted them, and shoved them back in. Things like this didn't happen in towns like Terra

Linda. Not in 2014. Maybe 1954, but sixty years later? No way.

Except this really was happening. And I was smack dab in the middle of it.

11

What I knew of the white supremacist groups came from documentaries about the KKK—horses and bonfires and men in hoods—and that movie my mom loved, *In the Heat of the Night*. In some unexamined part of my self, I thought stories like that were exaggerated, or at least extinct, dinosaurs of an old system. Both Mom and Beatrice were quick to assure me that racism now—at least most of the time—tended to be more subtle, harder for that, but also less violent. People were still killed because of their skin color, they said, but it was harder to prove that. "It's progress, I guess," Beatrice said, "but not much of it."

Yet, apparently, here in Terra Linda, my quiet town of 2,321 people, we had our very own white

supremacist group, listed with the Southern Pov-
erty Law Center map of Hate Groups and Everything. The White Citizens Council was homegrown
and very much alive, having survived the asteroid of
the Civil Rights Movement. A quick search on
Mom's phone told us that these groups existed all
over the South in particular. They were created in
response to the Brown vs. Board of Education decision to integrate schools. The members of White
Citizens' Councils were violent—if a little richer
than the KKK membership, Mom noted. Apparently, a Council member had killed Medgar Evers back
in the '60s, but Mom didn't share that with me. I
found out that fact when I did my own search later
that day.

According to Stephen Douglas, the Council
in Terra Linda had been around for decades and
had been started by two white business owners in
the 1950s when black-owned businesses started to
catch up with them in profits. In a small town like
ours, there really isn't room for two drugstores, but
Jim Crow made two drugstores necessary, and the
black drugstore was better—it had more things
people needed and cheaper prices—and these two
white business- men—Mr. Hollins and Mr. Rock-
et—did not much appreciate that. So they started a
hate campaign—flyers in mailboxes, rallies, boy-
cotts outside the store—and all the propaganda was
about how the black business owners were trying

to steal good, honest people's money and take it "back to Africa" or how the stores weren't clean or safe. They told the white women stories about how black men couldn't control themselves and might rape those white women in broad daylight right in the middle of the store. (The irony of this given what I now knew about the actions of slave owners was not lost on me.) There were bomb threats and fiery bottles through windows. Soon, the black drugstore dropped back in "its place" behind the white drugstore.

Once these men had a taste of power, they started a campaign to get all black-owned business-es out of the town limits, using the laws of Jim Crow to set ordinances that required proof of an-cestry to be able to purchase or lease storefronts on Main Street. Within a decade, every black-owned business in Terra Linda closed up.

Over time, the ranks of the White Citizens Council grew, bringing in bigots with all sorts of agendas—opposition to school integration and in-terracial dating in the '60s and then moving on to campaigns against "black music" in the '70s and subscribing to the "war on drugs" in the '80s—all to serve to keep white people in power and keep black people out of as much as possible. Mostly the things they did were quiet, subtle, managed be-hind the doors of the courthouse or local business meetings, so most people—including me, until now—didn't even know they existed, much less that they were still active.

But wait, let me clarify. Most *white* people didn't know, but when I asked Marcie about the Council after Stephen left the house that morning, she said, "Yeah, Mary, well, of course I knew. How could I not? They shut down my granddaddy's business. There are just things you don't talk about, you know?"

I tried not to be hurt by being closed out of this part of my friend's life. I tried to remember just what we were learning—that racism was still alive and well and that I was oblivious to it for the most part—but I was still a little bit sad. Racism as a system and a history kept my friend and me from sharing a perspective on the world, and that broke my heart.

I didn't have time to dwell on this sadness though because the last part of what Stephen told us made me so mad I could barely stand up. The latest actions of the Council involved the destruction of the Sutton Slave Cemetery because one of their members—Paul Douglas, Stephen's father—owned a construction company that wanted to win the contract. And just as Stephen had said, his dad knew about the cemetery and knew that preserving—or even moving—those graves would be a more expensive proposition. If they could simply destroy those graves, then their bid would be the lowest because they were the most local.

Yet, here we were, not only stopping their plans but also making a hullabaloo about it. "They aren't any too happy with you," Stephen had finished. "You just watch yourselves, and we'll do our best to prove that it was them, okay?"

Mom and I had nodded and walked Stephen to the door. By the time we got back to the kitchen table, the tension was sky-high. "We all know this isn't just about a low bid on the ball field, right?" Isaiah was standing, one hand cutting a slice through the air. He looked like a preacher with a mission. "We know that this has gotten personal because of what we shared about the Suttons."

I hated to admit it, but I thought Isaiah was probably right. Someone was really pissed off that we had talked about Maurice Sutton's repeated rape and fathering of children with one of his slaves. It was bad enough to talk about the Suttons as slave owners, but to bring up rape and children created by rape, that was unforgivable.

From the corner of my eye, I saw Shamila slip a long sheet of paper onto the table. She straightened it carefully, folding down the corner that had been bent. Then, she spoke in a volume just above breath, "I think there's something you guys should see." She pointed at the paper, and there, in the perfect lines of a family tree, was Maurice Sutton's line, and it ended with two names—Tina and Stephen Douglas.

I followed the names down the page: Maurice and Elizabeth, Julia Sutton and Benny McAdams, Mary Lee McAdams and Paul Douglas, David Douglas and Louisa Acock, parents of Tina and Stephen Douglas.

The Douglases were direct descendants of Elizabeth Perkins and Maurice Sutton.

Later that night, as Mom and I sat by the fireplace in the living room, a big bowl of popcorn in our laps and two cocoa mugs half-full of marshmallows at hand, I told Mom how Shamila had spent a lot of afternoons in the courthouse looking at wills and deeds and then many late nights looking at census records in order to put together this genealogy. It wasn't easy to do, but now we had solid proof of how David was descended from their great-grandfather and the woman he enslaved.

Mom said, "So Mr. Douglas must have known who was in the cemetery, and he must have thought that being descended from an enslaved woman would sully his reputation somehow. Right?"

It wasn't often that Mom asked my opinion on her theories, not because she didn't value it but because she could not do so in a session with a client. So when she did ask me, I tried to respond thoughtfully. I tucked my feet further under my legs. "I think so. It seems to me that this is a lot of trouble to go through just to save some money on a construction bid." I paused. "But people do crazy things for money . . . I'm just not sure they'd resort to open vandalism just to win a bid. *That* seems pretty over the top to me."

We sipped on our cocoa and stared into the fire. A stack of Tim Burton movies lay beside the DVD player, the between-holiday tradition we'd started a few years back when the fact of just the two of us had gotten a little hard as most of our friends spent these days with their families. Something about strange make-up and endearing but quirky characters gave us back a little of the shimmer that faded after Christmas.

As Mom slipped *The Nightmare Before Christmas* into the tray, I couldn't help but wonder what kind of hatred it took to not only want to destroy people's graves but to also make public threats against people you'd known your whole life. Mr. Douglas had coached my softball team one year, and Tina and I had been in school together since kindergarten. I just couldn't understand it.

But then, racism I didn't really get either. I mean, I understood what it looked like. Marcie had hateful things said to her all the time, not usually at school, but out in stores, especially if she was in her workout clothes. Something about a black woman in sweats and a hoodie set people off. And

I'd seen the way that people looked at the two of us when we were out together, sometimes like we were just an oddity, but sometimes like there was something wrong with what we were doing, a black girl and a white girl being friends. It just made no sense to me.

But then, from what I'd been reading online and in books Mr. Meade loaned me, that was the only predictable part of racism—the fact that it made no sense. All of it was based in fear: fear of people they didn't know, fear of a culture with which they were unfamiliar, fear of losing their power. That was a big one. When white privilege and white supremacy were threatened, people did crazy things. Like dig graves and put 126 Styrofoam gravestones in the yard of a local therapist and her daughter.

I got chills up my spine when I thought about what would have happened if Mom and I were black. It took me a long time to clear the image of burning crosses from in front of the TV screen.

12

Here's the part of the story I wish I could skip. I wish I could write some big heroic tale of how I was part of this great team who saved the day, how I sacrificed my own comfort—my own privilege in this case—to do the right thing. But I am not Tris or Katniss; I'm just Mary, and sometimes I am a big, stinking coward.

When we got back to school after the holiday break, everyone was sort of low-key—the short days, the cold temperatures, and a couple weeks of laying around and watching movies had tugged us all into a little bit of sluggishness.

Or in my case, it would have if I wasn't so scared. I spent the entire bus ride that first Monday back looking over my shoulder, afraid someone was going to come up and say something, watching carefully for strange cars out the windows who might throw a rock at me. It was ridiculous, I knew, but I couldn't help it.

In Mr. Meade's class, I'd read about the Freedom Rides, and I knew these things happened—and yes, I realized that those rides were intentionally designed to challenge the status quo and my regular thirty minutes on the big yellow machine wasn't the same, but still, I was scared.

Fear, as the White Citizens' Council reminded me in so many ways, was not rational.

I was able to kind of push my nervousness aside for a while in classes—we had tests coming up, and I knew I needed to at least pay attention so I could be sure I knew what I needed to review. Plus, it was fun to hear what everyone got for their holiday gifts. My best present was a set of Bose headphones to use with my phone. They were bright blue and perfect. But even they didn't block out my anxiety.

The morning was uneventful, but at lunch, fear climbed up the back of my throat like a hairy slug, and I lost any appetite I might have had. Javier noticed—we were still a thing, having gone out a few times over the break. He'd even come over for movie night with Mom and I once—and took my hand in his. "What's wrong?"

"What?! Oh, nothing. I'm just not very hungry."

Marcie heard me and spun around from her chat with Nicole. "You're not hungry? That only happens when you're upset. Spill!"

Just then, Tina Douglas walked by, and every muscle in my body tensed. She didn't say a word, just glowered and gave me a sort of smirk, and I felt like I was going to throw up.

"Oh no! You're not letting *her* get to you, are you?" Nicole asked, dropping her tray next to Marcie's.

"No, no, of course not." I gave a quick shake of my shoulders to shift the rising cold back down a few inches. "I'm just mad."

I was mad, livid in fact, but that wasn't the emotion that was making me seize up. Fortunately, after I forced myself to swallow a few mouthfuls, conversation swung back to gifts and the upcoming ski trip up at Massanutten. A bunch of folks were heading there—including Javier, Marcie, Nicole, and me—this weekend for a few hours. I wasn't much of a skier, but I did enjoy a good cup of cocoa by the fire with a book.

Just the thought of that day relaxed me, and I leaned back into Javier, who draped an arm across my shoulder. Yeah, that felt good.

The bell rang, and Marcie shouted over her shoulder. "I'll see you at the library for research after school."

That's when it happened, when my wimpiness shot through me. "Sorry, I can't come today. Mom and I have to take care of something."

Marcie shrugged and waved as she stepped into the throng leaving the cafeteria.

That afternoon, I took the bus home and was fully ensconced on the couch with a blanket, a bowl of popcorn, and a *Veronica Mars* marathon when Mom came out of her last appointment and plopped down beside me. "Whatcha doin'?"

Ah, the jig was up. This was Mom's casual way of noticing something was wrong and trying to get to the root of it.

I hadn't been home after school in months, and now, on the first day back, I wasn't just home, but I was full-out vegging on the sofa. Sure, I enjoyed my fair share of couch time, but not usually when I could be reading or, say, doing research on the Sutton slave cemetery.

"Nothing. Just felt like taking some time off."

"Oh, I would have thought the past two weeks would have served that purpose." I felt her look at my profile.

Sigh. I turned to look at her. "I just didn't feel like it, okay?" I could hear my voice getting louder, and with horror, I knew tears were close.

"Okay. But why didn't you feel like it?"

"I just didn't. Do I have to have a reason for everything?"

"Well, yes. We all do. But if you don't want to tell me yours, that's fine." She stood up and headed toward the kitchen. "I expect you'll be ready to go back by tomorrow. Spaghetti for dinner, okay?"

I nodded, but in a tiny, shiny cave at the back of my heart, I knew that I wouldn't be ready by tomorrow. I didn't want to be involved in this anymore, and that fact broke my heart.

The next morning, I lay in bed for as long as possible, long after Mom had gone downstairs, long after I heard the spatula in the frying pan flipping the bacon I could smell, long after I knew I should have been up, so when I finally dragged myself out of bed at the sound of Mom's footsteps on the stairs—the last time Mom had needed to come wake me up I was running a fever—I had just fifteen minutes to dress and eat before the bus arrived.

Mornings like this I was glad for ponytails.

As I jogged down the stairs, I tried to look chipper, which of course was my mistake because the Steele women couldn't really ever be described as "chipper." Mom took one look at me, glanced at the clock, and said, "Sit down."

I dropped into a kitchen chair and shoved a piece of bacon into my mouth. I might as well enjoy something about this moment because this lecture wasn't going to be pleasant.

"Mary Louise Steele, you are better than this. These people need your help, and because you are a little scared, you are backing off and acting like this is some great burden to you. Imagine what it must feel like to the people whose ancestors are buried in that cemetery—to see people want to destroy their graves for their own selfish reasons. What if someone wanted to do that to your Grandma and Papa's graves? How would you feel?"

I had thought of this all, of course. I knew I would be furious and hurt and scared if someone was trying to destroy my grandparents' graves. And I knew Mom was right. But I was just so scared. Scared of what people would say to me at school, yes, but more scared of what might happen to Mom and me if we kept going. I mean, they'd already torn up our whole yard—what would be next? Setting fire to the house?

Somehow, though, I couldn't tell Mom that. I just couldn't speak that fear to her. What if she thought I was ridiculous? So I said, "I know."

No two words make my mother angrier than "I know" said in a tone of resignation and apathy. For her, these are copouts, as if knowing a thing and accepting a thing are the same. I hear her all the time as she talks to her clients—"What do you know, then? And what are you going to do about it?" It's only in those moments that I ever hear her raise her voice to a patient.

"Get your backpack," she said. She grabbed her purse and fished out her keys. "Now."

I stood up as slowly as I dared and followed her out to the car. At first, I thought she was just so fed up with me that she was going to get me to school and out of her sight, the bus long gone down our road. But then, she whipped the car onto the side of the road by the cemetery and said, "Get out!"

Her long legs carried her to the heart of the graveyard quickly, her flannel bathrobe flapping in the wind. Yeah, she hadn't gotten dressed before she'd taken me on this mission.

"Moses, I can't hear you, but I suspect you are here." Mom looked around the cemetery with deliberate attention, and I saw Moses step forward from where he stood by his gravestone. "Mary is scared, Moses, because some people vandalized our house."   Seriously, how did she do that? I try to hide things from this woman, and it's useless. I might as well leave my sporadic diary on the dining room table for her to read.

"Moses, I suspect you know what it feels like to be frightened, and given what Mary has told me about you, I also suspect that you know something about doing what's right, even if it's scary. I'm hoping you can talk some sense into her."

At that, she whipped around and said, "I'll be in the car. Don't come back until you *really* know."

With a sigh, I walked over to Moses and sat down. The January ground was solid underneath my backside, and I could feel the cold seeping into my skin. But standing to receive this lesson didn't seem right somehow. So I sat at Moses's feet and looked up at him.

He smiled, and then his eyes got flinty. "Miss Mary, I know you is scared. And you probably should be. Isaiah told me what those people did to your house. That's not the work of kind people. But Miss Mary, as scared as you is, really that ain't nothing."

I could tell he was reaching into some sort of closed-off spot inside himself from the way his eyes slid into shadow. He was silent for a few minutes before he spoke again. "One summer night, so late that even the peepers had stopped singing, I heard the master coming into our house. Elizabeth was curled up against me sound asleep, but as soon as master's foot hit the doorframe, she was awake and standing up. I wanted to pull her back down to me, to cover her up while I stood to face that man, but she laid a soft hand on my shoulder and said, 'Shh' with just her breath. She knew—as I did—that if I fought, it would only make it worse."

"She had just reached him when he said, "Nah, Lizzie, not you. Where's Claudia?'" Moses took a shuddering breath. "Now, my daughter, *my daughter*," his teeth were clenched so hard I thought they would crack, "was just thirteen years old. She was sleeping with her sister on a cot beside the fireplace. She was just beginning to whisper about the boys around the farm, noticing how nice it was when they smiled at her. She was so pretty. Her eyes could make birds sing."

"When Master asked for her, I heard Elizabeth give a little whimper before she collapsed back on our bed. 'Nah, Master, please, no. I'll go. I'll show you a real nice time.'"

I tried to imagine what it would feel like for my mom to offer herself up in my place like that, to listen as still as I could in my bed while my mother tried to save me the same humiliation and terror she had experienced. I felt tears spring to my eyes.

"'Lizzie, why, thank you. That's very kind.' The man actually thought Elizabeth was doing him a favor!" The heat was rising in Moses's voice, and I could see his hands shaking. "'But no, I want Claudia. Now which one is she?'"

"I had one child whose existence that man did not taint with his foulness, and he wanted her. I was terrified for my girl, but I tried so hard to lie still, Miss Mary." He looked dead at me. "I tried. I knew that if I made a sound, Claudia—my baby—would only have it worse. But as he pushed his way through our beds, groping my children's bodies as he looked for hers, I pushed back all the fear, and I pushed back all warnings I could hear Elizabeth thinking to me, and stood up."

I could almost picture it—a father rising up from his bed in the dark, moonlight from the open window glinting off his cheekbone.

"'Now, Moses, this ain't no concern of yours.' Master took a step back when he saw me stand, but he didn't turn and go. 'You tell me where your girl is, boy.' I felt Elizabeth's hand tug on my arm, but I couldn't stop myself now. I reached up and grabbed him around the throat. I squeezed as hard as I could, but then, quick as lightning, my hands wouldn't squeeze anymore. And I was lying on the ground, looking up at Elizabeth. Then, I was watching all of them from over by the door. That's when I saw the pistol in Master's hand."

I wasn't holding back anymore. Tears were rolling down my cheeks, and I pulled my knees to my chest. "Moses," I whispered.

"I stood in that doorway and watched Master put his gun back in his belt and step over my body. I saw Elizabeth wailing over me, and I watched as Claudia stood slowly and walked toward Master. I had done all I could do, and it was not enough. "

"But just as I thought I'd lost Claudia, too, I heard Mistress coming running, a rifle under her arm. The gunshot had woken her, and she'd come out to see the racket. When she passed through me and saw my body there on the floor, the gun sticking out of her husband's pants, and his hand on Claudia's arm, she raised that rifle to her shoulder and said, 'Maurice, you let that child go. What have you done?' She kept that rifle on her husband and knelt down beside me close enough to feel that I was dead. 'Get out, Maurice. Now. Get out.' Master stared her hard in the face and then walked out the door."

"By then, all the other folks was in the yard, and Mistress told Ben and Leroy to lay me out on the table in the barn. 'Tomorrow, we'll have a proper service.' And they did. Everyone came to my graveside—including Master and Mistress—and they put my body in the ground. Here I stayed since."

I stood up as quickly as I could with the cold deep in my knees and hugged the man. I saw tears on his cheeks, but this time, he didn't try to hide them. "Moses, do you know what happened to Elizabeth and Claudia and your other children after that?"

"Yes'm. Elizabeth came by the day after they put me in the ground and said that Missus had hired her and all the kids out to the McKays just down the road. They were going to be the house staff there, and they'd have their own cabin and get half their wages to save."

"So your Mistress saved them?"

"Yes, Miss Mary, I suppose she did."

"Thank you, Moses. Thank you for telling me."

He gave me a quick nod, and I squeezed him one more time before walking to the car. I couldn't stop crying.

I probably don't need to say that I was at the Historical Society that afternoon, dipped deep in sadness by Moses's history and ready to bring justice through paper.

In fact, that was one thing this whole experience was teaching me—that sometimes the best way to find truth is to give it and that the truth given shines like sunshine on mold, killing anything secretive and false and hateful. That old cliché about the pen and the sword, yeah, that was true.

13

We were well into February before we got our next "big break" in the research. (I liked to say "big break" because it made me feel like Mariska Hargitay on *Law and Order: SVU*.) Shamila, the other members of the two genealogy teams—for the enslaved community and the Sutton family—and I had spent almost every weekday afternoon pouring over old newspapers, searching anyone named Sutton from Virginia on Ancestry.com, and interviewing old-timers from around town. Sometimes, on Saturdays, Shamila and I drove over to Richmond and looked through the records at the Virginia Historical Society and the Library of Virginia.

It was slow work—too slow for some of our team members, who Shamila and Mr. Meade decided might be better help with putting together the physical design of the family tree and a strategy for how to mark the cemetery itself than they would be on going through one more year of newspapers. I was glad of their decision because I was absolutely absorbed in this work but didn't want to show that to my classmates. I was already enough of a nerd.

Eventually, though, we were able to put together one fairly complete family tree that showed not only Maurice Sutton's ancestry and descendants but the Perkins family as well. The art team—as we now called them—took each name we confirmed and added it to a huge roll of paper tablecloth on which we were constructing the tree. So far, the tree stretched from one end of the Historical Society to the other, skirting through doors and ending up in the back room where Shamila's office and the archives were. When we measured it, it was fifty-two feet long.

We also connected some of the other enslaved families, people Moses would have known, as they married into the Perkins tree or were—forcefully—grafted onto the Suttons. In all, we had 403 names, all kin to one another in some way or another, and while the list was much more white than black, black people were not rare in this family.

As we compiled the names, the art team started to design a decorative tree that would hang on a display by the cemetery—the school carpentry class was building it, and they worked with students in the graphic design and computer science classes to design both the 3-D tree and the website for our research—called, at Mr. Meade's suggestion, *Branches and Roots: The Sutton Plantation's People.*

So we were actually feeling pretty good about things—the way the school was rallying around the project, the research itself, the lack of threats both verbal and physical—when we found what might have been the most significant document anyone in Malhalland County had ever seen, at least as far as I was concerned.

Given the public nature of this project, the Historical Society had been receiving a lot of donations—photographs, collections of yearbooks, old clothing, and papers, lots and lots of papers, most were family documents—old Bibles, report cards, baby books, and letters.

Many of these things were not relevant to our research since they were from families who lived in other parts of the county, but still, every time a new box arrived, I could see Shamila almost shiver with glee. This was what she lived for, after all—to do history for everyone, not just the wealthy, as has been the case for most of human history.

Since the bulk of these documents didn't relate to the Sutton slave cemetery and since that research was taking up all of Shamila's time beyond the regular assistance of society visitors, most of these new acquisitions were tagged and marked as "to be inventoried" in the back room.

So it's really odd—almost spooky—that one afternoon in early February, when an old man dropped off a box of papers, we started to go through them immediately. Maybe we opened this box because the man was black and most of the gifters had been white people. Maybe it was his sweet face, smooth as glass, and his slightly bent shoulders carried over his shuffling feet. Maybe it was that he was so sincere and quiet about his gift. "I thought you might keep these for my family. Hold our stories safe. Maybe you'll find something other people can use," he'd said.

Maybe it was just the way things went with this experience. Like I said, ghosts don't just appear to anybody, and neither do boxes full of important papers.

Most of the documents in this box were what you'd expect in a collection of personal papers. Titles to cars, old photographs, a few newspaper clippings. But there was also a bundle of letters, carefully tied with a teal, satin ribbon. On the top letter, it read:

J.O. Thompson
Charlottesville, VA

The writing belonged to a woman—slanted hard to the right and full of careful swoops. Probably eight letters made up the packet, and each was addressed the same way.

Shamila and I looked at each other quickly, and then she took the first letter out, eased it flat, and began to read:

June 2, 1872

My Dearest John,

The weather here in Terra Linda is fine today. The sky a blue so perfect that you'd think a blue jay painted it herself.

I and Mama are well, although of course her joints hurt her mighty bad. We have been trying to keep busy in the flower garden out back. The daisies are almost up to my shoulders, and the peonies have already blossomed out into their pink balls of fragrant fluff.

Most of our time, of course, is spent up at the Sutton place . . . .

Shamila's hands started to shake, and I leaned very close.

Mistress Sutton is not well, and with Master Sutton gone, well, it's just me and Tom to care for her and the house. She pays us fair though, and we don't want for anything if we need it. Still, I wish we could find other work. Perhaps in time . . . but then, I don't want to wish time away for that will mean that Mama is no longer with us.

Of course, then, I can come to you. I miss you so. I hope your studies are going well and that there isn't too much trouble with young Mr. Sutton sharing his books with you. I know the University would probably frown on *you learning, but I cannot help but think it perhaps the best thing in the world.*

We look forward to seeing you in July when you can take a break. Bring Mama a sweet if you would, and know always that you have my heart.

All my love,
Claudia

As Shamila read Claudia's name, I felt all the blood leave my fingers, and the strongest prickles of joy ran up my arms. I had to restrain myself from running all the way to the cemetery to tell Moses what we'd found.

But I wanted to know the whole story so I could tell him everything. Shamila and I carefully opened all the letters and read on.

When we were done, eight letters lay on the table, carefully spread out like drying candy swirls for the top of cupcakes. They really were that delicious.

The letters told the story of Claudia and John's brief separation while John attended a private medical tutorial in Charlottesville. His courses were taught by Maurice Sutton's son, Horace, in Horace's home, and John also lived there, at least that much we could ascertain about him from Claudia's words.

About Claudia, we learned far much more, of course. That she and Elizabeth were living back on the Sutton plantation, but now as hired help to care for the place and Mistress Sutton. Her brother, Tom, was there, too, and her other siblings—Elijah and Minerva—worked at the McKay place, still. She obviously had learned to read and write, and asked John to thank Horace for teaching her this skill.

But more than anything, we read one half of what must have been a great love affair because Claudia mentioned again and again John's letters, about how she so wished she could come there, too, as he'd asked, but that she needed to stay with her mother.

The letters spanned seven months, each letter sent near the first of each month, perhaps when someone was going into Charlottesville for a regular shopping trip, Shamila suggested. But the last letter came more quickly than the previous ones. It was dated December 26, 1872.

My Dearest John,

It is with the strangest mix of sorrow and joy that I write to tell you Tom and I will be arriving in Charlottesville by week's end.

Yesterday, Mama lay down on the bed in old Master Sutton's room after setting the night's fire. She had been tired of late, and her bones ached her so badly. I suppose she was just give out. Because when I went to check on her, I found she had gone out to Jesus. My heart aches with missing her.

Mistress Sutton passed over on Christmas Eve night. She died in her sleep, and she looked peaceful.

The two strongest women I have ever known have left this earth, one soon after the other, as if Mama knew Mistress Sutton might need her over there or maybe it was that Mama knew Mistress Sutton didn't need her anymore.

So you see, I am broken down by grief, and yet, once we hold the services and close up the house, Master McKay has offered to take us into Charlottesville to be with you. I cannot, then, be completely broken.

See you soon, my love.

Yours always,
Claudia

I could—in some tiny way—understand Claudia's feeling because here I was with the gift of these letters, and yet to share them with my friend Moses, I had to tell him about his wife's death.

Still, I knew that putting it off would only make it harder, so I asked Shamila if I could borrow the letters if I was very careful with them, and without hesitation, she slid them into a green folder and placed them in my hands. "Tell Moses I said 'Hello'."

Mom came a few minutes later to pick me up, and I quickly told her what we'd found and asked if we could please stop at the cemetery. She didn't even answer but drove straight there and sat in the car while I walked across to where I could see Moses standing.

"Where is Elizabeth buried, Moses?"

"Here, Miss Mary." He pointed to a low fieldstone just at his feet.

"Do you ever see her here?"

He shook his head. "And I don't wish I did. Even though I miss her something fierce."

I took a few steps closer and stood beside him, shoulder to shoulder. I followed his gaze to Elizabeth's stone and imagined his love for her was all wrapped up in the world of seeing. He stared at it softly with his lips lightly parted as if he hoped to breathe her in.

I slid the folder into his hands, surprised, and yet not, that he could hold it. "Open this."

He touched open the cover and stared, puzzled by the pages before him. He turned each page carefully, gently, studying the letters like they were the finest drawings. It was then—shame on me—that I realized he couldn't read. "Moses, these are letters from your daughter Claudia to her husband John O. Thompson."

Moses sat down hard on the ground, and I curled my legs under me as I sank next to him. "Do you want me to read them to you?"

He gave a slight nod, and I lifted one page from the stack, leaving the rest in his hands, where he washed his fingers over the words again and again.

We sat in that cold February air, and I read each letter, as Shamila had read them to me. When we got to the last one, I scooted just a bit closer, letting my shoulder brush his, and I read of Elizabeth's death and saw him smile.

"She always said she just wanted to feel one of those plush beds," he said.

Moses and I sat shoulder to shoulder on that winter afternoon, remembering.

14

At lunch the next day, I sat spinning my hair at my cheek, trying to figure out what to do about the letters. Shamila had suggested we could have another press conference and announce their existence, and Moses had said he would be okay with that. But both Mom and I felt some hesitation because, well, these letters were private love letters from people who had cared about each other deeply—and we didn't want their specialness to be tainted by the White Citizens Council or—perhaps worse—have people forget about them. Sometimes apathy is the worst crime.

When Javier slid into the table beside me, a quick kiss on the cheek before he shoved a huge forkful of salad into his mouth, I was startled and jumped. "Whoa, sorry. You okay?"

"Oh yeah, hey. Sorry, I'm just thinking about those letters." I'd told him all about them via text last night. "I'm not sure what to do."

"Well, I think the best thing to do then is to think about what you'd want someone to do if they found our letters." He blushed just a little.

We hadn't said "I love you" or anything, but things were getting more serious. And to have him compare our texts with Claudia's letters to John, I felt my knees wobble.

"So would you want someone to publish our letters if it might help to find out more about your dad's family?"

When he put it like that, I couldn't really say no, could I? If publishing notes that I sent Javier— notes that were truthful (if a little embarrassing) in their sweetness—meant that I might find my dad, well, yeah. I'd let them be published.

I gave Javier a kiss on the cheek and sat staring at him out the corner of my eye for the rest of lunch.

Mom and I had decided the night before that it was best to get everybody together and talk about what to do with the letters. Marcie couldn't make it because of a basketball game, but everyone else was in Mr. Meade's classroom at three thirty that day. Isaiah took off work early, and Mom asked her clients to move their appointments. Shamila came over from the Historical Society and brought Beatrice. Blanch stayed around to talk; he was a pretty set fixture at anything having to do with the cemetery, although he'd put a little distance between him and me since he knew that Javier and I were a couple.

Our conversation about the letters wasn't really that heated—actually, it was pretty clear what we were going to do from the get-go.

"I just don't know. Private love letters from a formerly enslaved woman to her boyfriend who is—probably illegally—studying medicine with his former master's son . . ." Isaiah sort of tapered off. I thought he had been going to say that these were personal documents, but by the time he fully expressed the profound reality of the letters, well, he seemed to convince himself.

Mr. Meade liked the idea of publishing them because then they became available for other people to study. "They'll help us understand more about the realities of life after Emancipation. Plus, the fact that Claudia and John could read and write is important in and of itself."

The meeting turned then to strategy. It was February 11th, so Javier suggested we do the press release on February 14th with a press conference at the cemetery that afternoon. The tie-in to Valentine's Day seemed too good to pass up.

We were just beginning to discuss how the letters would be published—newspaper, Historical Society newsletter, magazine article—when Blanch got a text and knocked over the desk as he stood up. "They're at the cemetery right now with a backhoe. Steve and Jamie are there getting in the way, but they don't think they could hold them off long."

It took us all a few seconds to react. The cemetery was protected—the school had put up a split- rail fence, and the display about the Sutton and Perkins family was set to go up in a few weeks. Everyone knew where the cemetery was, so why would someone try to destroy it now? Only heart-ache and court time would come if Mr. Douglas tried to tear up the graves at this point.

But those thoughts whizzed by as I grabbed my coat and scarf and bolted for the door, Javier close behind. I could hear Beatrice already on the phone to her cameraman, and Shamila was texting like mad as I breezed past her.

Javier and I made it to the site first, and al-ready, other kids had begun to gather. Steve and Jamie must have texted everyone they knew. They were standing in a semicircle, hands clasped, be-tween the backhoe and the gravestones. Twelve kids—some black, some white, some brown—putting themselves in the way of a huge yellow machine to save the bodies of people whose names they didn't even know.

I lost my breath and felt tears warm my cheeks.

I jumped right into the middle of the line and took two hands as Javier did the same with Mom, Isaiah, and Mr. Meade joining in, too.

"Kids, you have to move. This isn't your property, and we have been told to clear this piece of land," the backhoe driver said. He was a middle-aged white guy, maybe a little older than Mom, in a blaze orange cap, black jacket, and thick work gloves. He wasn't Mr. Douglas, but somehow, this man looked tougher, more staid. I didn't think he'd back down as easily.

"This isn't your land either, sir." I shouted. "This land belongs to our school, and this is a graveyard. By the law of Virginia . . ."

"Statute 57-38.1," Shamila shouted from her newly taken place in the circle.

"Statute 57-38.1, you cannot destroy graves without the express permission of the family members of those buried here. Do you have that permission?"

"Little girl, you are shouting out big words, but you don't know what you are doing. Of course, we have their permission. I gave it." The voice came from a large white man who had come up behind us and was standing in the middle of the cemetery. "This is my family's cemetery. My kin are buried here, and I've given permission for this cemetery to be destroyed."

By now, everyone had swung around, but despite the sudden turn of events, we held our hands tight.

"Who are you?" Mom shouted.

"I'm Maurice Sutton the fourth. My great-great-grandfather was the father of most of the people buried here, and I give permission."

From the corner of my eye, I saw Shamila almost drop her phone as she took a video. Here was a Sutton descendant who knew that his ancestor had raped enslaved women, and he was admitting it publicly. Shamila was smart to get that on record.

But just then, a large hand came from behind her and took her camera. "Ma'am, you are on private property, and we have not given you permission to film anything."

"Give me my camera back. This is public property, but that camera you're holding is *my* private possession." Shamila looked mad enough to use the scarf this third man was wearing to choke him until he gave her phone back. But he simply stepped away from her and tucked the phone in his pocket.

"Ms. Jones," the man in the graveyard said, "for the record, this is no longer public property. I bought it this morning. You see, the school board could not really refuse the sale of my own ancestor's graves, now could they?"

Something in the way he spoke made my skin tingle and a bad taste rise in my mouth. Then, I saw Mr. Douglas, Tina, and Stephen's father. He was standing just beyond the graveyard, smiling.

It all clicked then. Mr. Douglas had gone to find this man, this man who would not want to have his family name "sullied" with his ancestor's actions and probably even more by the idea of having black kin, and he'd recruited him to get his way. Now, not only could Mr. Douglas's business put in a lower bid on the ball fields, but the White Citizens' Council also got to wipe out another black historical site.

I felt like I was going to throw up.

"Now, if you'll kindly leave my property, I would appreciate it. As you can see, the police are already here, and they will arrest you if necessary."

On the road, behind Javier's car, I could see a police cruiser, and standing next to it—looking absolutely horrified—was Stephen. Poor guy, he really seemed upset. I could see his hands shaking.

But here is where all the evils of technology—its ever presence, our generations' addiction to it—are redeemed.   Everyone in the circle—including Isaiah and Mom—took out our phones and began Instagramming and Snapchatting and texting everyone we knew. I posted an image to Facebook of Maurice Sutton IV and labeled it "The man who is trying to destroy The Sutton Slave Cemetery." I saw Stephanie Miller's post come right after mine, a picture of the backhoe with the words "Get to the Sutton Slave Cemetery now. Help us save it."

The man who had Shamila's phone started grabbing at phones and shoving them into his pockets. When he got to Javier, my guy resisted, and the man grabbed him in a headlock as he tried to wrestle the phone away. I snapped a quick picture and shot it out over Facebook. "Help us. We're being attacked." Mr. Douglas wrenched my phone away.

They were too late. The News 28 van rolled up just then, and Beatrice and her cameraman were on the street in seconds, heeding the advice Shamila shouted—"Stay on the road. This is private property now."

Beatrice was fast on her feet. She had her microphone at the ready, and the cameraman started recording. "I'm here at the Sutton Slave Cemetery outside Terra Linda, where Mary Steele and her classmates from Terra Linda High School are putting their bodies on the line to save this historic place." She turned to me. "Mary, can you come over here and talk to us for a minute?"

I glanced at Mom, who gave me a quick nod, and the two people on either side of me quickly grasped each other's hand as I stepped out of the circle.

"Mary, what's happening here?"

"I'll tell you what's happening. Maurice Sutton—that man over there—is trying to destroy this cemetery—the cemetery where his ancestors are buried—because he's a racist coward."

"Mary, those are harsh accusations. Do you have any proof?"

"I do. Mr. Douglas, a member of the White Citizens' Council, is here." I pointed to where Mr. Douglas was, and he was gone. *Damn craven fool,* I thought.

"I don't see Mr. Douglas, Mary."

"He ran away when he thought he might be caught on camera."

Beatrice shook her head, trying to get me to quit, but I was too fired up.

Just then, I felt an arm brush mine, and Stephen Douglas, in his full uniform, was beside me. "My father was here earlier. But as Mary said, he left when the cameras came out. He is the president of the White Citizens' Council here in Terra Linda, and it's time that everyone knew it."

I heard a cheer go up from the crowd behind me as they saw Stephen come on camera, and for the second time that day, I felt tears on my cheeks.

People were awful quite a bit, but they were also beautiful and strong. I let Stephen wrap his arm around my shoulders, and we told the whole story together.

The rest of that week went by in a blur as news agencies from across the state caught word of the teenagers who had stopped the demolition of a historic cemetery and the member of the Board of Supervisors who was the leader of a white supremacist organization.

I did interviews with TV stations from Charlottesville and Roanoke and as far away as Washington, DC. Each segment showed all of us holding hands in front of the bulldozer and then interspersed clips from our cameras. The images left no doubt that not only was Maurice Sutton trying to purposefully destroy graves but that Mr. Douglas was spurring him on.

To say that school was a little less than normal might be my young life's largest understatement. I had some kids congratulating me with big slaps on the back and impromptu hugs in the hallway and others shooting me looks intended to carve out my heart.

I spent a good portion of Thursday afternoon with Mom, Isaiah, Mr. Meade, and Shamila in Principal McMahon's office as the school tried to figure out what, if anything, they needed to do. They had, indeed, sold the land to Maurice Sutton under the false impression that he was interested in preserving this part of the family cemetery. They had thought they were doing the right thing.

But now, of course, the backlash was swift. Parents wanted to know why the school board would want to destroy all the hard work their children had done for Mr. Meade's projects. The athletic boosters didn't understand why the school would want to allow a developer (Maurice Sutton was the CEO of a major housing company) to own land so close to the ball fields they were fundraising for. Community members were agitated on both sides; those who felt that Sutton had the right to do whatever he wanted and those who felt that those graves were sacred and needed to be saved.

Fortunately, we appeared to have the law on the side of the preservers. Virginia Statute 57-38.1 said that family members had to be informed, and Maurice Sutton was claiming that he was informed and could do what he wished with his land and the graves of his ancestors. But thanks to Moses—who had stood quietly beside Elizabeth's grave during the whole spectacle the day before—we knew that it was not just Sutton's ancestors buried there. For one, Moses was not kin to Sutton, and Moses had given us the list of other people buried there who did not share Sutton's genes.

The trick—again—was to figure out how to use this information without having to mention ghosts. Shamila spent all night Wednesday working, pouring through the rest of the box that had contained Claudia's letter, and she felt pretty certain that the man who had brought it in, Jesse O. Thompson, was the great-great-grandson of Claudia and John. The name fit, of course, but she hadn't gotten Jesse Thompson's phone number or address when he came in, so she was still trying to track him down.

The School Board issued a public statement—at our urging—saying that they fully supported the preservation of the Sutton Slave Cemetery and were deeply sorry that their choice to sell the cemetery to a direct descendant of the people buried there had nearly caused its destruction. "We are now working with the Historical Society and Tom Meade's junior history class to locate descendants of the other individuals buried in that cemetery. If you believe you are descended from people enslaved at the Sutton Plantation, please contact the Malhalland Historical Society."

As Mom and I drove home Thursday afternoon, we were both quiet, turned into our own thoughts even as Mom pulled over at the cemetery. I wanted to catch Moses up on things and spend a little time with him on the quiet.

I noticed Stephen Douglas's cruiser sitting just up the road and tossed a wave that way as I walked on. Judge MacIlvey had granted an injunction—at the urging of Stephen and the Historical Society Board—to protect the cemetery for the rest of February in order to establish, if possible, the identity of the other people buried there and contact their kin. We had fourteen days to do it, and in the meantime, the Terra Linda police would guard the cemetery 24/7 to enforce the injunction. That was a relief because I didn't really look forward to having to stand up against big machinery a third time.

I found Moses sitting at Elizabeth's grave, as I expected, but he wasn't alone. Next to him, a young woman knelt with her hands on her knees. She was black, probably in her twenties, and I'd never seen her before.

Moses looked up as I approached, but not wanting to alarm the woman, I didn't speak to him, just gave him a little nod. He smiled and then gestured toward her. "That's my great-great-great-granddaughter," he said.

The woman looked at him, grinned, and then turned to me. "That's right. I'm Josephine Johnson, and you must be Mary Steele. I'm glad to meet you."

15

I forced my feet out from under me before they went of their own free will and sat down beside Ms. Johnson. I kept looking at Moses and trying to communicate with my eyes to see if I was right—she could see him, too?—but he was enrapt in her, watching her face carefully, looking at her hands every time she laid them on the stone.

She caught me though—snatched my glance with one of hers—and said, "Yes, I can see him. Plain as you, I expect."

I must have looked like a trout, my mouth hanging open like that, because she said, "It's okay, Ms. Steele. I won't tell anyone."

I stammered into words. "Wha—oh, um, no, I'm not worried at you telling. It's just only Isaiah and I have been able to see Moses until now. So I'm just surprised, is all."

Isaiah and I had been spending a lot of time together of late; well, to be more precise, he and Mom were spending time together. While neither of them said anything, I suspected they were dating. Isaiah had quit coming for therapy right after he found out I could see Moses, too; the need gone, I guess, but he still came over—mostly for dinner now—and a couple of times, he and Mom had gone to movies and things. She seemed happy, and that made me happy.

He'd been coming to the cemetery, too, mostly just to sit and talk with Moses, to hear Moses's stories, to talk about the old times. That seemed to make him happy, which made Mom even happier, and my slightly grumpy natural demeanor meant I had to show I was overjoyed, because I really was excited for them.

Ms. Johnson said, "Oh yes, Moses was telling me about Isaiah, our cousin."

If I hadn't been sitting down, I would have fallen to the ground again. "Your cousin?"

"Oh, you didn't know? Right. Well, Isaiah is the great-great-grandson of Tom Perkins, the brother of my great-great-grandmother, Claudia. So cousins."

I stared at Moses with my now becoming standard slack-jawed expression. "Moses, does Isaiah know?"

"No, ma'am. I haven't told him yet. Not sure he's ready to realize he's kin to Maurice Sutton—the first or the fourth either."

Moses had a point. I would certainly struggle if I learned that my family included rapists and racists. "Moses, how did you know?"

Ms. Johnson settled back and stretched her legs in front of her. "Granddaddy, maybe Mary needs to know now?"

He looked at her, his eyes soft, and then he turned his gaze to me.

"Moses? What's going on? What do I need to know?" I swiveled my head from side to side, staring at first Moses then Ms. Johnson and back again.

Moses stepped closer to me and laid his hand on my shoulder. "Mary, I knew Moses was Isaiah's kin same way as I knew you were Minerva's. I can see it in you. "

I felt the air swim in front of me and Moses's hand on the space between my shoulder blades. I tried to take deep breaths, but I couldn't find oxygen. I had to lay down. So I did, right there in the cemetery, with a ghost and a woman I'd just met watching over me.

They sat silent, staring out at the mountains across the valley, while my mind raced . . . how was this possible? I'm not black. My mom's not black. None of my family is black. Surely, we would look "black", right? But even as I asked these questions, I knew the answers—no, we weren't black, but our ancestors might have been, just like Maurice Sutton IV's. The color of skin says nothing about a person's ancestral past. Shamila reminded me of that again and again.

Later, I knew I would have to deal with how I thought about "race," pushing into the what I now knew about race not being a real thing but just something people created to keep other people "in their place," and decide how that affected my identity.

But now, now I was moving on to think of kin. . . I was kin to Claudia and Tom and to Elizabeth and Elijah. And I was kin to Maurice Sutton. He was my four times great-grandfather. Just the thought of that made my stomach roil.

Then, I realized, I was kin to Ms. Johnson right there, too, and I sat up and took her hand where it sat in the grass beside me. Oh, oh, I was kin to Isaiah, but the thrill of that epiphany was short-lived . . . oh no, Mom was dating her cousin.

Moses must have seen my face fall because he leaned closer, "What is it, girl?"

"Oh, it's just that Isaiah and Mom are dating, and well . . . "

"Rest, child, you're not kin to Isaiah through your mama. I don't see Elizabeth in her."

It took me just a moment. If I wasn't kin to Minerva through Mom . . . I gasped.

The first thing I learned about my dad, and it was that I already knew most of his extended family. I felt like I needed to lie down again.

I must have sat in that field for a good bit while Moses and Josephine talked. (I figured I could probably call her by her first name now since we were cousins and all.) I tried to listen to what they were saying, but I couldn't get my mind to work quite right. I kept thinking about being kin to Isaiah and to Elizabeth, about how much it disgusted me to be descended from Maurice Sutton the first and a cousin to the fourth, about how nice it was for the family to be more than just Mom and me now.

But mostly, I thought about my dad. Would he look at all like Isaiah? Was he light-skinned or dark-skinned? Did he look like me? Was he tall and lean like Moses, or short like I was? I had so many questions about him, questions that I really hadn't thought to ask before because he felt like a total absence, like someone had made a cardboard cutout of a man, painted it like a shadow, and set it in my life.

I hadn't ever known where to begin asking before. Now, I had one piece of his story, as if all the background behind his shadow was getting filled in, and the desire to know more felt like it might climb out my ears.

Later, I would realize that this feeling must have been just a taste of what Josephine and Isaiah and every other African American person I knew felt when they found something about their ancestors. A void for so long—barely shaped with the shadows of stories, the lingering voices carried through generations of vocal chords—now beginning to fill with names and places. Yet, even then I knew that my white skin would mean that I could find most of my stories—including my and my dad's stories—so much more easily.

A horn beeped out at the road; Mom was back from the grocery store. I waved her over and heard the car shut off. She threw Stephen Douglas a wave, too, and came over to where we were sitting. I did the introductions and told Mom where Moses was—no one wanted to accidentally step or sit on him—and asked her to sit down.

"Mom, Josephine is Isaiah's cousin."

The tilt in Mom's head and her smile were full. Yep, she was a little giddy over this man. "Well, isn't that lovely?"

"Mom, um, so am I?" I didn't mean for it to be a question. I knew Moses would never lie to me, and I had no reason to doubt Josephine's story. But my whole life, I had looked to my mom for the nod that told me what was truth and what was lie, what was good and what was bad. I needed her to give me that nod again.

Her head tilted to the left this time, as it did when she was thinking, and she said, "Yes, I suppose that's possible. Your dad was from here in Terra Linda, so why not?"

Well, I mean, she'd told me she loved him, that he was excited about me, and that he'd died before I was born. Beyond that, she hadn't been willing to say anything at all.

I still couldn't tell you just what brought me to tears . . . that I missed my dad, that I now had a connection to him, that we had a huge family and maybe could do holidays for more than two? Probably all of it. And once those tears started, I couldn't stop.

I heard Mom tell Josephine and Moses—she spoke to the air somewhere near his right shoulder—that she had probably better get me home. Mom put her arm around me and turned me toward the car.

Moses leaned down and whispered in my ear . . . "I'm so glad to call you family, Miss Mary."

The kindness of those words brought the wave of tears harder, and I smiled at him before I walked away.

Once I was in my Eeyore pajama pants and the comfiest old "Farm Fair" t-shirt I owned, Mom brought me tea, and we folded up together on the couch. She reminded me everything she knew about my dad.

His name was Joseph Stills, and they met one night in the town library. He was there tutoring some kids, and she was picking up her weekly supply of Interlibrary Loan materials so she could finish up her PhD. Mom said that she liked the look of him right from the start—he was tall and stocky, in a big plaid shirt and jeans, and he was leaning over a young boy, talking him through long division. They exchanged numbers and had their first date right downtown at the Skylight Diner.

From then on, they were together. He worked down at the plant during the day—the same plant where Isaiah was a manager now—and after work, he tutored the kids she saw in the library as part of a program started by the YMCA in Lexington. He told her he'd grown up poor and that school was very hard for him . . . so he thought he might help these kids get just a little bit more ahead of where he was so that they could do more than work a factory line if they wanted. "If I hadn't already been falling in love with him, I would have when he said, 'if they wanted.' He wasn't out to change the world, or make anybody live the way he thought they should. He just wanted to prop open a few more doors for these kids if they wanted to walk through them."

They dated for just six months and then got married in August in a quiet civil ceremony downtown. Mom had suggested their church—*our* church—but Dad wasn't much for organized religion. Their honeymoon was just a night over at a bed and breakfast in Lexington. Mom had to finish up her dissertation, and Dad wanted to save his vacation time. They planned to take a trip across country the next year.

"We never got to make that trip. Your dad was at work one day when a steel press went offline. The foreman told me that your dad must have thought his partner had turned off the machine, because he climbed right up on it to clear the jam and as he did, the machine began to work again . . . "

Like she did every time she told this story, she was crying.

"He never came home."

We sat holding hands under that blanket for a good while before Mom spoke again. "But two days before, I had told him I was pregnant with you, and he was so excited. He ran out immediately and bought all these tiny little clothes and shoes. And that stuffed bear, the one on the corner of your bookshelf, he bought that, too. He would be so proud of you."

I smiled at Mom and sat quietly with her for a few minutes, the familiar story still sad even in this, probably the hundredth telling. Now, though, a new question came to mind.

"Mom, did you ever know his family?"

"No, Mary, I didn't. Apparently, he had some sort of falling out with them, and he never talked about them at all. I actually thought they probably lived far away. I'm sorry, Mary."

I nodded. I wanted to stay there, lay on that sofa and fall asleep like I had when I was a little girl.

But this wasn't a little girl's story.

I hugged Mom, kissed her cheek, and climbed to my bed, where I cried myself to sleep in the quiet whisper of a winter's night.

When I woke up, the sadness of the previous night had sunk into a hollow space in my belly. I wasn't exactly happy, but I wasn't debilitated either. In some ways, I was even a little excited. I had a family, a big family.

That movie *Dan in Real Life* had always made me want to have a big family who gathered at the holidays, who did goofy things together, made each other angry, and then forgave each other in a massive mixture of hugs and shrugs. While I realized that probably wasn't going to happen with the Johnsons, Washingtons, and Perkins, still, it was kind of nice to imagine a giant touch football game with all my cousins.

Javier, clearly prompted by Mom, picked me up that morning, and when I sat down in the car, he leaned over and wrapped me in a tight hug.

At school, I only had a minute or two at lunch to tell Marcie what had happened, but she reacted just like a good friend should—with a hug and a "that sucks" about Maurice Sutton and the perfect amount of excitement about the fact that I was kin to Elizabeth. Then, she brought me back to the task at hand. "Mary, you do realize this means you are a descendant of people buried in that cemetery."

I gave her that look that says, "Yeah?! Haven't you been paying attention?"

"No, Mary, listen. You can protest the demolition of the cemetery. You have that right now."

I leaned back hard in my plastic seat. She was right. I could. In all the excitement about my new family members, I had forgotten.

I could take Maurice Sutton head-on now.

Sometimes, it feels really good to turn sorrow into righteous action.

After school, I ran as fast I could—a light jog that turned into a brisk walk that turned into a saunter—to the Historical Society. I caught Shamila up as fast as possible, and she knew just what we needed to do. We had my family tree to build.

It didn't take us long. Unlike the ancestries of African American people, European American genealogies are usually a little easier to trace, and mine was much simpler because I not only had a person to start with—Elizabeth Perkins, and someone to trace to—my dad, Joseph Stills.

We started working backwards from my dad to his parents, Martha and Matthias Stills, and then to their parents, and so on. I wasn't sure which line led from Elizabeth to my dad, so we had to trace them all. Even in just four generations, my father's family grew to thirty people who were his direct ancestors: my grandparents, great-grandparents, great-great-grandparents (Minerva and her husband Louis among them), and three times great-grandparents. Thank goodness Minerva listed her actual parents on her marriage certificate—Maurice Sutton and Elizabeth Perkins—or we would never have been able to prove my connection to the cemetery.

Shamila printed copies of all the documents, and quickly faxed them all with a cover letter—signed by me and her—to the Virginia Department of Historic Resources, the government office in charge of cemeteries. Then, she clipped four more copies together; one for me to keep, one for Mom, one for her to lock into a fireproof box here, just in case, and one to send certified mail to Maurice Sutton IV.

We hoped he would simply back down when he saw we had a direct descendant to challenge his claim to the graves, but neither of us was confident. So we spent the rest of the evening compiling Isaiah's genealogy—with him consulting on the phone—and after a quick text from him to Josephine Johnson, we had her permission to put hers together.

It was well into the early hours of Thursday morning before we finished. I could barely see straight after so many hours of scanning old documents, but I was still exhilarated. Now, we had three direct lines to people buried in the cemetery—all to Elizabeth, of course—but that should not matter. What mattered is that Maurice Sutton had a fight on his hands, a fight generations old.

We were determined to win it.

16

Mom was a firm believer in good attendance, so despite the fact that I hadn't gotten home until after 3:00 a.m., she still came bustling into my room to pull off the covers and get me upright before seven o'clock the next morning. I'm fairly sure I made it to the bus with my eyes closed.

But once the energy of our research penetrated my sleep deprivation, I was wide-awake and buzzing. I found Mr. Meade just before second period and told him the news in a quick hallway whisper, and at lunch, I filled Marcie, Nicole, and Javier in on our family—it still felt weird to say that—ancestral lines, and the plan that Shamila and I had hatched for stopping Maurice Sutton.

Unfortunately, the lack of sleep made me a little less cautious than necessary, and it wasn't until I had blabbed almost everything that I saw Tina was standing just behind Marcie and listening to every word. Her face was as red as a rooster comb, and I thought I could see her hands shaking at her sides.

Javier must have noticed her about the same time I did because he was on his feet already when she lunged across the table at me. With a swift hook of his arm, he pinned her to the table and called the teacher on duty over. "Tina tried to choke Mary, Ms. MacDowell. I had to restrain her." His tone was completely innocent and light, even though I could see the considerable strength it was requiring for him to hold Tina down.

Ms. MacDowell acted swiftly and with the full power of the lunch monitor, whisking Tina up by her arm and off through the cafeteria doors toward the principal's office.

I was startled but not scared this time, and four hours of sleep was bringing the giggles up quickly. Javier gave me a quick peck on the cheek, and Marcie and I laughed all the way down the hall.

I texted Mom from fifth period, and by the time the final bell rang, she and Isaiah were standing by the door to the bus lot, waiting to pick me up. "We're on our way to meet Beatrice," Mom said as she swung the door open. "It's show time again, girl."

Mom hadn't wasted a second after I told her that Tina knew what was happening and would probably get word to her father. A third press conference was scheduled for the cemetery this afternoon at 4:00 p.m., but first, Beatrice wanted to get interviews with Josephine, Isaiah, and me . . .

I realized with a start that I hadn't had a chance yet to tell Isaiah what was happening and jumped forward to grab his arm where he sat next to Mom in the front seat.

"Isaiah, I need to tell you something."

He placed his fingers over mine and turned to look at me. "Mary, Moses told me last night when I stopped by to see him. But I think I already knew before that. There had to be a reason that you and I were showing up in that graveyard, right? When your mom told me that you had found your dad's ancestors were related to Elizabeth, I figured that must be the ticket. So it's all good, cousin." He squeezed my hand and turned back in his seat.

"Oh, good." That was a relief. "Um, and you don't mind being related to me when you and Mom . . . ." I trailed off because, well, I didn't really know what to call it. Were Mom and Isaiah going out? Dating? What do old people call this thing? "Seeing someone"?

Mom caught my eye in the rearview mirror. "Isaiah and I are dating, Mary. And *do* you mind, Isaiah?" She flicked her glance over to him.

"Not a bit. I figure it just gives you one more reason to keep me around a little longer."

From the back seat, I saw his shoulder move toward her and watched as his fingers interlaced with hers.

I grinned to myself as Mom took the turn up the mountain.

The scene was different at the cemetery this time. The road wasn't lined with cars. In fact, aside from the police cruiser nearby, the only vehicles in sight were Beatrice's news van and a little convertible car, Josephine's, I assumed.

"We thought it might be better for this one if it was a more solemn event," Isaiah said. "Josephine, you and I will simply tell the stories of our families while we stand by Elizabeth's gravestone. And we'll share a bit about what it means to know our family histories. Sound okay?"

I nodded, but I was actually kind of worried that I'd be able to talk about my dad on camera without crying.

Beatrice and Josephine joined us as we walked across the cemetery, and we all did introductions. I saw Moses watching us from across the graveyard. He gave me a nod.

Then, Beatrice said, "I'd like to walk and talk with each of you for a few minutes on camera. I want to build an intimate story here, one not just about the cemetery but about the people associated with it. I think we can do that best one on one, okay?"

She started with Josephine, and as they walked slowly between the stones, Miles, the cameraman, followed them at a distance. Beatrice and Isaiah did the same, and then it was my turn.

"Mary, tell me what you've learned this week about your personal connection to this cemetery."

I took a deep breath, and before I even began to speak, I felt the tears spill over. "This week, I found out that I am descended from Elizabeth Perkins on my dad's side."

Beatrice laid her hand on my arm. "Your mom never told you about his family?"

"She couldn't. She didn't know them. But I'm very glad to know I have a broader family, and I'm totally honored to be Elizabeth Perkin's great-great-great-granddaughter." I looked over to where Moses stood nearby and saw he was smiling.

As we walked back to join the rest of the group, I wiped my eyes quickly with the back of my hand just in time to notice Javier, Marcie, and Nicole standing quietly by Javier's car. He gave me a small wave, and I smiled.

Beatrice lined us up in a semicircle around Elizabeth's unmarked gravestone. We weren't, of course, going to tell anyone that we knew this to be Elizabeth's stone. We didn't have any documents to prove that, and announcing that a ghost told us might be a credibility killer. Still, it felt right to stand near our great-grandmother, to have her place close while we claimed this land for her and for us.

Shamila arrived with the documents we'd copied last night, and she handed us each a stack of papers with all the proof we needed to establish our claim. Then, beside us, she set up an easel and propped an image with three lines on it—one connecting each of us to Elizabeth. It was a lovely piece of art—simple with its condensed family trees and beautiful—a white oak like those around us now watermarked onto the background, and soft faces of black and white people rimming the border. "I am having full family trees like this made for each of you," Shamila whispered to me as she handed me my papers.

On Beatrice's cue, Isaiah spoke directly to the camera. "I am the great-great-great-grandson of Elizabeth Perkins. She is buried here, in the Sutton Slave Cemetery, in an unmarked grave." He gestured with a sweep of his hand just over Elizabeth's grave. "I am joined today by two of Elizabeth's other descendants—Josephine Johnson and Mary Steele. We have just discovered our linked ancestry because of a generous donation Mr. John

Thompson made to the Malhalland Historical Society. The letters of Claudia Perkins Johnson gave us the clue we needed to tell the story of our link to this place."

He knelt down beside Elizabeth's gravestone. "We do not know the names of everyone who is buried here, but we hope—in time—to discover those names so that more people can know the sacred ground where their ancestors rest. This is why we must stop Maurice Sutton from breaking the law, yes, but also from breaking the sacred trust of what it is to be human. As human beings, our greatest calling is to care for one another and to respect the stories each of us tells. These stories are wrapped back, cords into the past that tie us to all of our people who have walked before us and ribbons into the future that tie us to the children, grandchildren, and great-grandchildren we do not yet know. When we disrupt a cemetery—because of expediency, expense, or embarrassment," Isaiah laid long on that last word, "we say to all around us, your legacy does not matter; therefore, you do not matter. We must do better."

As he rose, the cameraman moved to Josephine. "I am the three times great-granddaughter of Elizabeth Perkins, two times great-granddaughter of Claudia, great-granddaughter of Elise, granddaughter of Harriet, daughter of Adele. I come from a long line of strong, brave women. I am the three times great-granddaughter of Maurice

Sutton the first, two times of John, great-granddaughter of Michael, granddaughter of Terrance, daughter of Ralph. Maurice Sutton was a cowardly, abusive man, but he is mine to claim. The men who lead from him to me have sought to make right and do right. I do the same and call on Maurice Sutton the fourth to step out from under his ancestor's legacy and embrace the roots of his family tree that are not rotten." Josephine's face was hard and her eyes wide. "I call on you to join us, cousin, and claim the good that is your family name."

My turn. I took a deep breath. "I have never known my father. He died before I was born, and so I have never had much of his story to claim. Until now. My father—Joseph Stills—was the great-great-grandson of Elizabeth Perkins, which makes me cousin to Isaiah, Josephine, and Maurice Sutton. My father was a kind and generous man, spurred by something in his spirit to do good for the people around him. I hope I am making him proud by standing here today." I looked up at Moses, and his smile broke the last barrier of facade on my face, and the tears rolled.

I continued, "I have found my family here in this place—not just my father, but my cousins, my grandparents, my aunts and uncles. They rest here in this sacred ground—quiet but strong and true as they were in life. I did not know them either. I couldn't tell you what they looked like or how their voices sounded. But I can tell you something of their character because they survived one of the most horrible experiences a human can have—to be owned, controlled, abused, and discarded by other people. My three times great-grandmother Elizabeth survived rape and humiliation to raise four strong and powerful children, including my great-great-grandmother Minerva. Elizabeth's strength, Minerva's strength gave me life. I cannot repay that debt." I paused and took a deep breath and spoke with a ferocity I didn't know lived behind my tongue. "But I *can* and *will* honor their lives by protecting their resting place with all that I have. Maurice Sutton, join us . . . or be prepared to fight."

I felt Josephine take my hand and looked to see Isaiah take hers. We were all crying now.

That evening, when the story aired on the six o'clock news, I was surprised to note that I could see—just when I looked with my eyes unfocused—an entire line of people with their hands clasped, standing behind us. Elizabeth—I don't know how I knew it was her—at the center of them all.

I woke up the next morning when someone was pounding on our front door. It was barely light, so I knew I hadn't overslept . . . and I could hear Mom's bedroom door close—she had still been asleep, too. Early indeed.

I threw on my robe and ran down after Mom. She was standing at the door with her arms spread across it, a very angry Maurice Sutton trying to push his way through the doorframe.

My phone was in my hand, as it always was, so I snapped a quick picture, and the flash turned his attention to me.

"Oh no, not again. You're not putting my picture out there again. Give me that phone." Mom held her ground as I sent the picture via Instagram—"Help!" as the caption—and texted Isaiah. Then, I joined her at the door as we pushed it shut and locked the deadbolt.

It felt a little like one of those horror movies where the young woman runs around trying to be sure that all the other doors were locked. Mom and I scurried to first the garage and then the back door. Everything was locked up tight, but that didn't make us feel much better. Windows were still breakable.

I ran upstairs and jumped on my computer, sending out Facebook messages as fast I could—the typewriter a much more efficient means than my phone's face. As I returned to Mom, I could see Maurice Sutton talking with several men, including Paul Douglas, at the edge of our yard. All of them were in suit pants with button-down shirts, like they'd stopped to do a little harassment on the way to the office.

As I watched, I saw a sleek gray car pull to the sidewalk, and a man I had never seen stepped out. He was wearing a full suit and his hair was perfectly coifed. In his hands, he had a packet of papers. Maybe it was too many episodes of *Law and Order*, but I knew immediately that those were legal documents of some sort.

"Call a lawyer, Mom," I shouted as I blazed down the stairs. "We're going to need one."

Just then, the doorbell rang. Mom and I glanced at each other, and then, she opened the door. No way to avoid it, we figured.

The man in the suit stood there. "Mary Steele?" He looked at me.

"Yes?"

"You have been cited with a restraining order. You are not to go within one hundred feet of the Sutton Cemetery, Maurice Sutton, or any of his residences."

I stood at the front door, my hands braced on both sides of the frame, and watched the man in the suit walk away.

As I glanced over, I saw Maurice Sutton snap my picture, a wide grin on his face.

I wasn't really a vengeful person, but I knew he would regret that image almost immediately. And not because I was in my Eeyore p.j.'s.

17

By the time I watched the school bus drive by, Mom's lawyer, Mr. Thomas, was in our living room, as were Isaiah and Josephine, who had also been issued restraining orders. Mr. Thomas had reviewed all our paperwork carefully and said, "He has no cause for this. None at all. I don't know what judge issued these orders, but these are totally bogus."

It didn't take us long to learn that Judge Hostler was a member of the White Citizen's Council. Stephen Douglas confirmed that suspicion and told us he'd talk to the District Attorney and see what they could do. If I hadn't felt like I was on a *Law and Order* episode before, I did now.

Josephine, I was quickly learning, was funny, very funny. She cracked jokes at her own expense and at the ridiculousness of our situation—"Yep, small town living. The newspaper needed a front page story, so they issued restraining orders against the people who had *been* threatened. We'll have our mug shots on the *Terra Linda Review* next Wednesday, if they can fill enough pages to make the paper fold."

Isaiah smiled at her and leaned way back in his chair with his legs outstretched. "If they come to arrest us, Mary, just remember, don't accept water or soda from anyone. They offer beverages so that then you have to pee and will confess more quickly if they refuse," he said with his eyes closed.

At least we could laugh. But inside, I was exhausted and furious. While Mr. Thomas talked with Stephen, the district attorney's office, and finally Maurice Sutton's attorney, I texted Marcie. She was wise to my anger and after expressing the requisite dismay and anger, spent most of her end of our conversation saying things like, "I understand, but you have to calm down." and "I hear that. Mary, though, you have to think now. Think."

Within a couple of hours, Mr. Thomas had contacted a judge in a neighboring town and had a 2:00 p.m. appointment to get the restraining orders rescinded and to discuss the ramifications of filing criminal charges against Judge Hostler, a tactic that would be used more as a threat than an actual course of action. None of us were up for a real legal battle, but we were also not content to let the judge's and Sutton's actions go unchallenged.

The five of us piled into Mom's car and drove to the Skylight Diner. Nothing sounded better than a big cheese omelette, some greasy home fries, and toast made soft with butter. I had missed breakfast, and we needed a plan.

Mr. Thomas explained the case leveled in the restraining order against us. "Sutton has claimed that he feels unsafe in your presence and that he fears you will do damage to his family cemetery. He also states that you have slandered him, which means that he is saying you have lied about his actions with the intent to make him look bad publicly.

"We did intend to make him look bad in public. That was the point. But we never threatened him with any harm, and we certainly wouldn't hurt the cemetery. The more this goes on the more I want to . . . ." I was having a hard time not shouting, and I felt my hand ball into a fist. Mom handed me another piece of toast and a packet of strawberry jelly. I busied myself with slathering, taking her hint.

"But we didn't lie," Isaiah said. "Everything we said is the absolute truth. He is trying to destroy the cemetery. He is doing it because he's ashamed . . . "

Mr. Thomas interrupted. "That may be, but where the slander comes in is that you claimed he is breaking the law. Is that true?"

"Yes." Mr. Meade spoke from behind the lawyer's shoulder as he pulled up a chair. "Yes, Maurice Sutton is breaking the law. According to Virginia Statute 58-3.1, anyone wanting to disrupt the ground of a cemetery has to make a good faith effort to locate the descendants of the people buried there and obtain their permission for such action. Maurice Sutton made no such effort—if he had, he would have easily found out you were descendants, right?" Mr. Meade looked at Isaiah, then Josephine, then me.

We looked at each other. Maybe it was time to tell everyone about Moses. After all, he was the one who had put us on the trail of Elizabeth's children, who had told us that Maurice Sutton the first fathered them.

At Isaiah's nod, I was about to open my mouth and tell the whole story, when Shamila walked in.

"Come with me. I have someone you need to meet."

Mom threw some cash on the table, and I waved goodbye to the pile of hash browns still on my plate.

The look on Shamila's face—jaw set and eyes bright—told me this was worth the loss of a few fried potatoes.

As we walked down the block to the Historical Society offices, for the first time, I wondered exactly how we were going to prove that Elizabeth Perkins was buried in that cemetery. I had been operating on what I knew was fact because Moses told me, but it was only now I realized that only three people in the world could see Moses. And we were the three people accused of slander.

(The accusation still stood, fueled by a press conference Maurice Sutton held for the Noon news cycle, but Mr. Thomas had succeeding in having the restraining orders lifted and the records expunged. The judge in Lexington had laughed out loud, apparently, when Mr. Thomas showed him the charges.)

As I approached the Historical Society door, I wondered—again—if I was insane, legitimately insane. After all, I was claiming to be descended from enslaved black people and their white enslaver, all based on the word of a man who died over 150 years ago. When I thought of it like that, I almost understood where Maurice Sutton was coming from.

Almost.

But the truth of the matter was that people I trusted—people who I knew loved me—believed me. They trusted what Isaiah, Josephine, and I said about Moses and Elizabeth. If I couldn't trust myself, surely I could trust them, right?

This path of thinking—the one that would lead to insanity if I wasn't already there—was cut short when we walked into the Historical Society offices. An old white man sat in the chair behind Shamila's desk, his feet outstretched and his hands folded across his stomach. I thought he might have been napping, but his eyes snapped open as soon as Shamila spoke his name.

"Mr. Sutton, I'd like you to meet . . . ." She introduced us all one by one, and the man stood and shook each of our hands.

"Nice to meet you, everyone. I'm Maurice Sutton the third. I think I may have something you could use."

It took me a minute to process who this was. . . Maurice Sutton the fourth's father and Maurice Sutton the first's grandson. Holy moly poly.

We followed Shamila and Mr. Sutton into the reading room and pulled chairs around the central table. The old man took a piece of folded paper out of his breast pocket and laid it smooth on the table. Then, he slid the paper to Isaiah at his right. "Please read."

Isaiah studied the top of the page, which I could see included handwriting and looked quite old. "The Slave Cemetery on Walnut Ridge."

I heard a gasp and realized it was my own breath leaving my lungs.

Isaiah continued. "Scipio - 1822. Mariah - 1832. Old Hannah - 1835. Ezekiel - 1842. Letty - 1848. Nelson - Age 12 - 1853. Moses - 1858." Here, he paused, and when he continued, his voice shook. "Lissa - 1861. Elizabeth - 1872."

I felt my hands grasping the edge of the table and realized I was trying very hard to stay upright.   When I looked at Josephine, her face mirrored mine with its tears.   Here, here, was a map—tiny hand-drawn rectangles marking each grave—of our ancestors' resting places.   Here was proof, but here, too, was recognition.

I don't know just how long we sat in silence—awe and grief and gratefulness filling the room—but it was Josephine that spoke first. "Mr. Sutton, thank you."

The man pulled himself upright with some effort.   "My dear, this is simply your due. I deserve no thanks.   It is I who should be thanking you for all the work your family did to give my family the life we have lived."   His eyes filled.   "I am deeply ashamed of what my family has done to yours, and if I knew how to make it right, I would.   But I can make right what my son is doing, and I hope this helps."

If air could gain mass, it did right then, filling all the space.   It would take me a lot of time to recognize that moment for what it was—the grace of healing that comes when truth is spoken and truth is heard.

Isaiah reached over and laid his hand on Sutton's. I put my head on Mom's shoulder beside me. "This is what it's like to have a family," I whispered.

We stayed in that room for a long time that afternoon, telling stories. Mr. Sutton offered to give all of us a tour of the farmhouse and the outbuildings. The slave quarters had long ago been torn down, so we couldn't see Moses and Elizabeth's house. But Sutton knew where the houses had been and said he'd show us. Isaiah walked Mo—as he told us all to call him—through each of our genealogies, filling in the spaces of our shared family story. It felt good, hard but good.

Then, Mr. Meade brought us back to our central issue at hand. "Mr. Sutton, Mo, I'm just curious, and you can say you'd prefer not to answer if you'd like, but why is your son so determined to destroy this cemetery?"

"I wish I had a good answer for you, Tom." Mo slid his hand back over his white hair. "It's a hard thing to own up to your family's history. That's part of it. To accept responsibility for what your ancestors did. To come out of that acceptance with a willingness to change and to not let the shame harden you. It's taken me eighty-six years to get there, and it's still hard."

"But for Maurice, I think there's more. Some greed, of course. He wants those new fields to carry his name. He's told me that. But mostly, I think it's fear. Some people call that hate—racism, I mean. He doesn't like black people." Mo smiled at the black faces in the room. "I don't know. Maybe fear and hate are one and the same. But it's that, mostly. Just plain ugliness, if you ask me."

Somehow, still, I had been thinking there would be another answer—something that justified the hatefulness that this man's son had been throwing around—some personal injury done to him that he could not get past maybe, some misguided effort at good will for the school . . . something other than what I had known all along was really the case. The man was letting his racism control him, pure and simple.

I felt like crying all over again.

We spent a long time together that afternoon, hearing from Mo, telling our stories, grafting together—family, blood, and friend. By the end of that day, we had a new plan. This one didn't include a press conference or a public meeting. This time, we would use coffee and conversation and a tiny handheld camera.

Our lawyer, Mr. Thomas, made all the arrangements. We needed to be sure we were protected, yes, but we also wanted Mr. Sutton to think we were capitulating. It was the only way we figured we could get him in the same room with us. Our suggestion was that we meet on neutral ground, in the conference room at the local library. It was semiprivate space where we could talk candidly, but it also provided some level of protection because we were in a public space.

Marcie and Nicole took the afternoon off from their respective practices to be present, and Javier asked his boss at the pharmacy for a few hours so he could come, too. They, Mr. Meade, and Shamila would be stationed around the library, ready to call for help, report to Facebook, or lend their physical presence if needed.

Josephine, Isaiah, Mom, Mr. Thomas, and I would be in the meeting as the defendants. Every time Mr. Thomas called us defendants, I felt like Judge Judy might walk in. And I felt icky.

Maurice Sutton would come with his lawyer, too. The plan was for us to discuss the issues at hand, share our evidence of kinship, and come to an amicable accord about next steps. Okay, that was the pretend plan. None of us really thought that would work.

The real plan, the one we figured we'd get to right quick, was that we'd show our evidence, and Maurice Sutton would claim it a fake. Things would escalate. He would accuse us of slander again, and we would challenge him to prove our allegations of racist action—"hate crime" was the term that Mr. Thomas said we should use—were false. He would be unable to do so, so he would resort to claiming we had no proof of kinship and, thus, no claim. Then, we'd nail him with the cemetery plot Mo gave us—the document we'd conveniently notarized with Mo's signature earlier in the day.

It was going to be a tough meeting; we all knew it, but we figured by 5:00 p.m., this would all be sorted, charges dropped, cemetery safe.

You can see what's coming, right? Yeah, I figured.

Everyone arrived right on time—3:30 p.m. I could see Marcie and Nicole in the comfy chairs by the window with magazines in hand. Javier was hanging out by the videos, and Mr. Meade and Shamila were set up with laptops beside the mystery novels. Mom came in her best "I mean business" suit, and I was even wearing a skirt. Josephine and Isaiah had both just come from work, so they were donned in their business attire. We looked pretty spiffy.

But clearly, we were taking this meeting more seriously than Maurice Sutton. He came in wearing mud-spattered jeans, a baseball cap, and a flannel shirt with a long rip down one sleeve. Just the sight of him made my skin crawl.

The door had barely closed when Sutton said, "Alright, I have cows in the field. Let's get this over with. You're wrong. Stop, or I'll take you to court and get everything you own."

I was glad to see that Mr. Thomas had started the camera as soon as we walked in. He calmly said, "For the sake of record, this conversation is being recorded. Now, what evidence do you have of my clients' wrong-doing, Mr. Sutton?"

Sutton looked at his lawyer, and the quiet man—who at least had the respectability to wear a suit—pulled out papers and began to list the times we had trespassed on Sutton's land, the disruption of construction that I and our gathering had caused on two occasions, and most recently our accusations that Sutton was planning to dig up the graveyard out of racism.

Mr. Thomas was ready, though, with the state statutes on access to burial grounds, the law requiring proper exhumation and movement of the bodies, and the documentation of our genealogies.

As expected, Sutton challenged our kinship to anyone in the graveyard. "No one knows who's buried there, so how could you know you're kin to them?" He was starting to shout.

With as much flourish as I could muster given that I was nearly shaking with anger, I laid Mo's cemetery plot on the table. "Your dad gave us this document. " I let him stare at the plot for a second, even pick it up. We had the original in a file and multiple copies with multiple people, just in case.

Mr. Thomas continued. "As you'll see, this document, dated November 25, 1875, lists the names of all the people buried in that cemetery and is signed by Maurice Sutton the second, your grandfather, I believe, sir. Here," he pointed with the tip of his pen, "you'll see the name of Elizabeth Perkins, Ms. Johnson's, Mr. Washington's, and Ms. Steele's three times great-grandmother. You'll also see, here, Moses Perkins, Ms. Johnson's three times great-grandfather. So clearly, they are kin to people in that cemetery."

I could see the red climbing Sutton's neck. It was about to get loud in here.

But Mr. Thomas didn't let him get a word in. "Additionally, since you yourself have claimed kinship to the individuals there, you have accepted the family story that Maurice Sutton the first, your three times great-grandfather, had a relationship with Elizabeth Perkins. Thus, you have already acknowledged—on camera—your kinship to the people in this room, sir." Mr. Thomas never raised his voice, but wow, did he know how to send in a zinger.

"Thus, our business here is concluded. While my clients could easily charge you with slander, returning the treatment you have given to them, they would rather invite you to be a part of their new Sutton Slave Cemetery Committee and get your input on how you all preserve your ancestor's graves."

And that was it . . . that camel-breaking straw . . . an act of kindness, undeserved and unwanted, sent Sutton right over the top. He stood and threw the table up against us.

All the papers and the camera went flying to the floor with a crash. Mr. Thomas and Josephine had been able to scramble out of the way from their places at the end of the table, but Isaiah, Mom, and I were pinned. And Sutton was getting closer and closer.

From the corner of my eye, I could see Javier at the door, and I gave him a quick shake of the head. Marcie and Nicole stood next to him, their phone cameras on the glass, recording it all.

Sutton was so enraged he didn't even notice them there. I was glad of that—we'd have record— but I was also terrified. His hands were clawed and moving closer and closer to Isaiah's throat. I wasn't sure we'd be able to get him off if he grabbed hold.

Javier—wise man that he was—ignored my shake off and plunged through the door, setting the table upright as he moved toward Sutton. Marcie and Nicole were right behind him. Their entrance was enough to distract Sutton from us, and that slight shift of focus gave Mom just the time she needed. She stepped up to Sutton, spread her feet wide, and assumed a boxing position.

Now, let me say that my mom is not exactly what you'd call an athlete. She's lean and healthy, but she's not much of a workout fan. And boxing, yeah, she's never boxed in her life.

But she has bluffed a lot, showing confidence with her patients even when she's not sure of the way forward. And here she was, fists raised, all the power she could muster into her bluff.

I spent one terrifying second thinking Mom might hit him. Okay, I spent one exhilarated second thinking Mom might hit him, and then a terrifying second. Sutton was out of control, and I was sure that if Mom landed a blow, he would level her.

Fortunately, his lawyer got hold of his arm and stepped between Sutton and Mom. Sutton's eyes cleared just a bit, and he stepped back.

I knew what Mom's analysis would be of this moment—that man had major problems with anger management. But the tension settled like a sheet falling onto a freshly-made bed, and Mom took a step back.

Mr. Thomas looked at Sutton's lawyer, Mr. Hoover, and said, "So we're all good?"

Mr. Hoover took a long look at his client. "Yes, we're good. All charges will be dropped."

We slowly filed out of the room, Mr. Meade and Shamila joining the procession as we passed out of the library. This didn't look much like a victory celebration, even though I suppose, on some level, it was. This felt more like the aftermath of a battle, and I wasn't sure anyone had really won in that room.

At the diner in town—the place was quickly becoming our headquarters—we regrouped over burgers and milkshakes. My hand was shaking where it held Javier's under the table, and I felt like I could cry at any moment. Josephine and Nicole looked a bit unsteady, too, and Shamila and Mr. Meade—once they got the whole story of what had happened—flushed with anger. Mom, though, Mom was very, very quiet.

Lots of suggestions were thrown out—put the video on YouTube, share the video with the police, press formal charges for assault—but no one seemed to have much energy behind those ideas. Somehow, striking back at Sutton—as much as that appealed to some dark part of me—didn't feel good or useful.

If I'd seen one thing in that room, it was the man's fear. His eyes were bugged with it. Mom had taught me well enough that fear does not respond well to threats. It just entrenches itself and puts up more walls.

When Mom spoke, she put words to just what I was thinking. "We need to return evil with good." Or as I thought, *we were going to have to go all MLK on his ass.*

Here, I expect you're thinking that we're wimping out, we're letting ourselves be beaten, we're not fighting for what's right. I hear that, I do, and I get what you're saying. But this lesson, learned when I was seventeen, has stuck with me all my life. You don't have to fight with harm. You can fight with good, too.

By the time we left the diner, we were all exhausted, the sun had long ago set, and we had a potluck meal to throw in Sutton's honor in just three   days.

18

I expect in bigger cities or more "fancy" communities the idea of throwing a potluck might have seemed quaint and cheap—that's what Stu, the kid from New York said when I invited him. "Okay," he said, "That's stupid. You throw a party and you make the people you invite bring the food. Totally lame," but I'm translating.

Still, here, a potluck is what you do with people you love and trust—folks from church, your extended family, the people who live on your street. It's a sign that you not only care enough to get together but you also know that putting together food for that many people is hard on one person. Also, it shows you trust each other enough to eat any number of varieties of casserole, which is to say you trust them a lot.

So Isaiah called the fire chief, explained what was happening, and reserved the fire hall. We had to bump a baby shower from the meeting room, but the chief said she was still three weeks from her due date so she'd make it. Small town love and practicality all in one.

We put the word out on Facebook, of course, and printed up some postcards to hand out, each notice titled "Support the Sutton Slave Cemetery. Bring a dish and learn how you can help." Posters hung in every business in town by Thursday night, and Beatrice got a plug on the station's public service announcements. I even heard the event on 97.5 WTLA on the way to school on Friday.

It was going to be a big time. We'd arranged to have a bouncy house in the parking lot, and the kids from 4-H were bringing over their animals for a mock petting zoo. Javier and The Screaming Lizards would play for the event, too.

By last period Friday afternoon, the buzz was pretty strong. I could hear people talking about what their parents were bringing and wondering how many desserts they'd have to pick from. As I headed to Javier's car, I got a lot of "See you tomorrow night, Mary," and by the time I dropped into his bucket seat, I was wiped out. I'd spent the

whole day talking things up and answering questions—no, there would not be a dunk tank; it's February. Yes, it would be great if you want to set up a
temporary basketball hoop in the parking lot. That I
just wanted to go home and sleep. But that wasn't
an option. We had last minute plans to make.

Javier drove slow as we crossed town to the
diner. We'd been together long enough for him to
know that this much activity both made me really
excited and drained the energy from every cell in
my body. He held my hand, kissed it as he parked,
and draped his arm around my shoulders for comfort as we walked in.

Mom and Isaiah were at our usual table in
the corner, their fingers intertwined. When they
saw us, they pulled away from each other. I was
too tired to feign I hadn't seen, so I said, "Okay, seriously, we know you're dating. It's totally fine if
you hold hands."

They looked at each other and smiled that
dopey smile of love, but they didn't hold hands, at
least not where I could see, which was fine. I had
bigger fish to fry.

The central component of our plan was
based on the supposition that Maurice Sutton
would be so livid that we were throwing a big
shindig that he'd show up to disrupt it in any way
he could. We expected a full turnout of the White
Citizens' Council and then some. But we were
ready. Stephen Douglas and other police officers

would be there just to keep things civil, and we'd have video cameras around the room to capture anything that might go wrong.

But our hope was that any malice would be thwarted by the big "Thank You Mr. Sutton" banner that would hang from the front of the firehouse.   Marcie and Nicole had made it the night before on a huge piece of white canvas, and they'd be in the bunk room of the firehouse to unfurl it as soon as we saw Sutton round the corner.   Javier would be our lookout.

So yeah, not just a potluck, right? More a stakeout of love.

Our hope—naive and idealistic for sure— was that Sutton would see the banner, slow his progress, and come in to find that the entire celebration was in his honor. A cake with his name on it.   Thank you notes from all the guests.   And a small ceremony where we'd thank him for rallying us so effectively to the cause of saving his family cemetery.

Of course, this was the height of irony because, well, he didn't want to rally us and yet he had.   That expression "All press is good press" is true.

Because the fact of the matter is that if Sutton hadn't caused so much of a stir, we might have still saved the cemetery, but most people would have forgotten about it in two months. Now, Terra

Linda had formed a bulwark around that little place and the people buried there.

Plus, now we knew we had some real work on racial reconciliation to do in our little town, and as Mom says, the only way to heal things is to look them square in the face.

Saturday came both two years and two minutes later. On some selfish, tired level, I just wanted it to be done—the meal served, the gesture of reconciliation offered, equilibrium, or its facade, returned. But mostly, I just wanted it to go well—for us to have a good turnout, for Sutton to be surprised into kindness, for people to bring at least two kinds of macaroni and cheese for me to choose from.

We spent every waking hour doing interviews locally and nationally—the cemetery had gotten a bit of national news coverage when one of our cousins in Ohio contacted her local TV station—corresponding with more of our cousins and picking them up from the airport and train station; and preparing decorations. Fortunately, Mr. Meade had enlisted our class to help again, so they were managing most of the pick-ups and decorations. If they hadn't been, I wouldn't have been able to steal away on Friday afternoon to see Moses.

I missed my friend, and while I was sure that Josephine and Isaiah were also stopping by to give him updates, I wanted to be sure for myself that he was okay with what was happening. I didn't want to be doing anything—particularly given how his life had ended—without his full awareness and consent.

So when the bus dropped me off at the market just up the road, I almost ran all the way into his arms. He didn't hesitate to wrap me in a hug so tight I felt like my spine might crack. The further we'd gotten into our work with Moses's family and saving the cemetery, the more physically present Moses began to appear to me. He looked almost completely solid now, and his hugs felt full as any I'd received from a living person.

We sat down in our usual spot, and I looked at him, a little nervousness spreading across my chest. "So Josephine and Isaiah told you, right?"

He nodded.

"And you're okay with it? I mean, you're okay with us inviting Sutton and trying to make things right?"

He nodded again.

"Because this doesn't mean that what he's done is okay or that what his great-great-grandfather did to Elizabeth and then to you is okay."

Moses just stared at me.

"I mean, I'm not sure it's good to forget. I think we actually need to remember and forgive.

Otherwise, then, well, what are we really forgiving anyway? Where's the power in that? Seems to me that we need to look the pain right in the face, let it hurt and then let it go by saying, 'What you did was not okay. But I forgive you because I need to.'"

I paused and looked at my friend closely. He met my eye. "I need to," I whispered.

"Yes, Mary. You do. I'm not a bitter man, but I carried this load for a long time, never knowing quite how to put it down. It ate at me, twisted my heart. But when I started to feel like I was ugly as anything Maurice Sutton did, I knew I'd crossed a line. I let it go a long while back." He let out a long breath. "But I'll never forget."

I looked at my hands for a long time before I spoke. "Moses?" I looked up into his soft face. "Thank you."

"For what?"

"Thank you for letting me see you. I know you did that on purpose."

He smiled. "So you figured that out, huh? I wondered when you would."

"Yeah, I figured that if God is merciful and just then the least God could do would be to let a man who never had any choice in his life or death be able to choose how he walked the earth after."

He looked out across the field. "I suppose that may be right, Mary. That may be right."

I scooted over next to him and lay my head on his shoulder. He draped his arm around me, and I nestled in. "Can I call you Papa?" I had wanted to ask this question for a long time now.

"I wish you would." I felt his arm tighten on my elbow. "I wish you would, child."

19

On Saturday afternoon, the camera crews and reporters arrived first for a press conference about the cemetery. We were announcing our plans for the monument there, and Shamila was sharing the news that an anonymous donor had given $10,000 to the Historical Society so that they could digitize as many of the personal family collections as possible. The work would mean that those documents could be available to anyone in the world via the Internet.

We showed mock-ups of the monument, and Shamila brought one of Claudia's letters, used with Josephine and Moses's permission, to show on camera. Twenty-five or thirty newspapers and radio and TV stations were on hand, and after Isaiah and Shamila made our two brief announcements, we took questions for about forty-five minutes. Some of the greatest interest came when Mr. Meade responded to a question about student involvement with an announcement that the local history work we'd done here had led him to propose and have approved a new course in local history for next year. I was as surprised and excited as anyone to hear that.

We finally just had to wrap up the questions by urging all the news crews to stay, eat, and be on alert. We had one more big event planned for the evening.

As cameras dropped from shoulders and pens were tucked in pockets, we grouped together on the stage. It was time to put our plan in motion. Javier headed up the road to watch for Sutton, and Marcie and Nicole took their places upstairs. Mom and I took our stations by the food tables to help people lay out their dishes and get drinks while Isaiah and Josephine opened the doors to the huge crowd we'd been hearing gather outside.

Soon, the room was full – two hundred or more people had arrived with far more than two macaroni and cheese options. Within minutes, the bouncy house was full, and the folks from Mr. Meade's class were working their volunteer rotation to keep kids safe and to prevent "bouncy hogging." The Screaming Lizards were also on stage, doing some quiet background music as cover for their lead singer on lookout. People were eating, and the girls from Marcie's basketball team were painting faces. Someone I didn't know was tying balloon animals in the corner.

It looked like everything was going really well. A big town party—perfect.

Then, I heard Marcie's whistle from upstairs that told us the banner was dropped and Sutton was on his way.

Mom and I quickly climbed to the stage, Isaiah and Josephine in front of us. Shamila and Mr. Meade came forward, too, and Nicole and Marcie arrived a few seconds before Javier came flying in the door.

By now, the crowd realized something was happening and had turned toward us. Isaiah took the microphone and said, "Folks, we need your help for a big surprise tonight. On the count of three, we will all say, 'Welcome, Mr. Sutton.' We want him to know we are glad he's here. Can you help?"

A few puzzled looks passed between friends and families, but most people just looked at him and nodded. We all turned toward the door.

The door opened and three large white men entered, Mr. Sutton first with the other two flanking him from behind, as if they were his bodyguards, and maybe they were. Each of them was in a standard business casual outfit—khaki pants, button-down shirt—and Sutton in particular had that look a man gets when he's just shaved fresh—all shiny and smooth.

They strode into the room without hesitation, and we responded in turn. "One, two, three!." Isaiah practically shouted into the microphone.

A huge voice erupted together. "Welcome, Mr. Sutton." And the crowd broke into applause, more for their ability to follow directions than because of Sutton, I suspected.

My eyes were on Sutton, "Keep your friends close, and your enemies closer." That cliché flashed through my mind unbidden. I'm sure my face was not welcoming, so I forced myself to smile and said again into the mic Isaiah handed me, "Welcome to our celebration in your honor, Mr. Sutton. Because of your efforts," I paused here for irony, I guess, "we have found our families, and our community has come together in new ways. We thank you for that." I was surprised to feel a lump in my throat.

Sutton was surprised, too, if the raised hands and braced posture were any indication. He had come to disrupt this gathering—no one doubted that—but here was welcome instead of anger. Not exactly the Civil Rights Movement's sit-ins, but definitely a bit of meeting hate with love here.

I felt like we had done our part. We'd brought him here, we'd greeted him with warmth, and now, he could eat and mingle with everyone else. I planned to go say hello—Javier nearby—and then enjoy the rest of the night, Sutton neutralized.

But Isaiah had different ideas, ideas we had not discussed.

He put out his hand for the mic, and with a furrow in my brow, I handed it over. "Mr. Sutton, we really are glad you're here. We have a few things to say to you."

Oh no, I thought. *Isaiah's anger has bested him. He's going to lay it all out, and we're going to have a fight on our hands.*

"Thank you, Mr. Sutton, for being true to what you believe and think. As much as I find racism abhorrent, as much as at times your words and actions have felt like a rope around my neck, I am choosing to put aside my own anger and hate as best I can and choosing instead to try and understand. In some ways, you are the bravest person here because you said publicly what many people," he looked right at Mr. Douglas, who had slid into the corner of the room, "believe and act on in secret. By putting your fear—it has to be fear that drives that kind of hate—out in the open, we can heal it. Or at least I hope we can."

People were shifting a little, the truth of Isaiah's words sliding home for many, I expected. But it was Isaiah's next sentence that made my heart pound.

"Mr. Sutton, would you like to say a few words?"

I couldn't believe it. It was one thing to hold a party for the man, to make a banner; it was another entirely to give the hatefulness a microphone. I looked at Josephine, and I could see that she shared much of my feelings. Stephen Douglas had moved closer to the stage, I noticed, too.

Sutton glanced around him and saw the faces of the town—his town—wide open with expectation. At that point, it seemed to me he had two choices: walk back out the door or come up on the stage. To his credit, he didn't run.

As he climbed the risers to the stage, I felt Javier take my hand and glanced over to see that Mom had joined Isaiah with Mr. Meade and Shamila by Josephine.

Isaiah handed Sutton the mic, and in that split second, I hoped for about a million things: tears of repentance, polite commentary on the event, or even hateful words that would prove us—me—righteous in my anger. But Sutton began with, "I realize that most of you think I'm wrong. That I'm a hateful old man, and you may be right. But here's the thing . . . blacks and whites, we just ain't the same. We don't talk the same. We don't like the same music. We don't live the same."

I felt my chest tightening. In some small part of me, I had been hoping for redemption, for repentance, for some miraculous change of heart. But I have always been a hopeful, idealistic person.

"I think maybe y'all are right. Maybe I'm just old-fashioned and backwards, but I don't think we should be proud of being descended from ni—from blacks. I just don't. So you can tell me all you want that my great-granddaddy might have loved those mixed kids of his, but I don't believe it. I won't. And that's just the way it is."

When I looked out over the people of our town, some were crying. Some had jaws set like glaciers. Some had their mouths open, their hands at their sides, rage in their eyes. They were, in fact, mirroring all that I was feeling in that moment.

I had expected some sort of scene—a chair thrown, harsh words slung about, maybe a quick departure on Sutton's part. But I had not expected blatant hate.

I was still naïve, too hopeful to protect my own heart.

The rest of the evening moved along as you'd expect a small town gathering to go, but with an achy pall over the whole space. A child jumped on another child in the bouncy house, and the EMTs on hand had to do a quick wrap for a sprained wrist. The gossip mill got going pretty quick about Sutton, and since he had stormed off stage after handing the mic back to Isaiah, gossip was all we really had.

I did see that Blanch was talking in the corner with one of Marcie's teammates, Cheryl, and I might have imagined it but thought they touched hands once. Sometimes hope sparks in tiny corners.

I stayed on the sidelines a lot, ducking in and out of the kitchen to refill dip trays and my reserve of energy. It felt like something heavy and soft had shifted just a bit, a hay bale of hate rolled a little toward the cliff, maybe. Perhaps what we had needed was to just throw the hate into the middle of the room and all stare at it. Maybe Sutton had given us that gift, painful though it was.

By the time the fire hall cleared, I was exhausted and sad. So, so sad.

To be honest, though, the real hard work came in the weeks following Sutton's speech. Now, we had this man who we knew hated some of us, and it took a great deal of fortitude for everyone—but especially for Isaiah, Josephine, Shamila, and Marcie—to stay cordial with him.

Since the Sutton Cemetery had made national news, we also got a fair share of looky-loos, folks who thought that somehow a five-minute broadcast while they ate their spaghetti gave them a right to come and tell us what to do in our town. Protesters showed up at Maurice Sutton's office, and we had to spend some long days trying to scrub hateful words off of some of the stones in the graveyard. Hate doesn't just scrub out though. It stains.

But we stayed at it, and in time, things got better—as they are wont to do. The historic panel got placed at the cemetery—with images of some of Claudia's letters, a photo of Maurice Sutton the first, and a list of all the people in the cemetery front and center with Moses's name on the top. That alone felt like victory.

We got a split-rail fence around the cemetery, too, and Shamila made sure all the appropriate county and state records were updated with the exact location of the graves. She said that we knew we'd had some success when a volunteer from a website called Find-A-Grave contacted her about coming to take photos of the headstones so that they could go online for researchers.

In town itself, things were icy for a while—tensions high, suspicions higher. The White Citizens' Council went even more underground than usual. Stephen told us that his dad had left the potluck incensed, determined to entrench himself in his hate further. Occasionally, we saw evidence of their efforts— an ordinance coming through the Board of Supervisors that would have made rental properties illegal in the town limits, effectively forcing all the poorer people in town (many of whom were black) to leave. But mostly, people were wise to their game, and Stephen kept a close eye on things for us.

Mom and Isaiah coordinated a series of "conversations" about race, racism, slavery, and white privilege that were well-attended by towns-people. Each conversation began with a brief presentation by an expert who gave an overview on the topic—i.e., race itself is a myth but the effects of that myth are profound; white privilege is almost impossible for white people to see, and yet, we have to try. Then, they would open the floor to questions and stories. Sometimes the conversations were quite heated—the white privilege one was particularly hard for our mostly white town—but as long as people abided by the two rules of that space, "Speak the truth," and "Respect other people's experiences and lives." Mom and Isaiah let people talk. I think they helped everyone; I know they helped me.

Javier and I kept dating, going along at our quiet pace. I'd go to The Screaming Lizards shows; he'd read at the Historical Society while I continued researching the Perkins family, my family. That was easy and good. And the same seemed to be true for Marcie and Nicole and for Isaiah and Mom, too. The man basically lived at my house now, and I liked that because Mom was happy . . . and because I had kind of missed having a dad.

Most Saturdays, I spent some of the day over at the cemetery picking up fallen branches and composting the wilted flowers that came to the headstones regularly now. For a while, Moses kept me company. We'd walk and talk, and he'd tell me the good stories of his childhood—the time his brother Junius threw him in the pond when they were fishing, or the way his mom made biscuits so soft that you could stick your thumb in them and fill that hole with molasses. We grew even closer then, Moses and I. Often, we walked hand in hand as we chatted. I loved that man.

But I knew our time together would not last forever or rather, I knew Moses was only still here because I wanted him to be. "I done my part, Mary," he said one day. "I always wondered why I felt like I needed to stay. I never understood it, but I knew that I had to be here for some reason."

"Moses, you mean you could have left? You could have gone to be with Elizabeth?" I felt the tears on my cheeks. "I always thought you were trapped here."

"Oh no, girl. I could have left a long time ago, but see, that didn't feel right. I still had some- thing I needed to do. So I stayed. Sometimes that's all there is to do—stay right there til that moment comes."

I understood that in my young way. I did know.

Then, one day, when I came to the cemetery, he was gone. I knew it as soon as I arrived. The air just felt different—emptier. I walked over to his gravestone and caught a tiny whiff of pipe smoke. There, by the stone, a pink piece of quartz glittered.

As I bent down to pick it up, I heard Moses speak one more time. "Mary, child, I'll see you in just a little while."

I folded that stone into my hand and walked home.

Acknowledgments

My deepest thanks to all the many people who have helped me with this book. You are far too numerous to name, and yet, I appreciate each of you.

A special word of thanks to my Book Peeps, the world's greatest launch team who advised, goaded, and cheered this book into print. Thank you.

A special thanks to my friends in the work of recovering the stories and relationships of enslaved people—the members of the Central Virginia History Researchers, the Louisa African Americans Research team, the Louisa County Historical Society, and the members of Coming to the Table.

Huge heart-thanks to my father, who has championed every word I have ever written. And the biggest words and love to Philip, my partner, my first reader, my love, and my biggest supporter always. I love you.

Discussion Questions

If you are interested in talking about this with a class, a youth group, a book club, or any other gathering, I would be *thrilled*. Here are a few questions to get y'all started.

1. What do you know about your town's history with slavery, racism, or civil rights?

2. What people or situations in your life did you think about when you were reading *Steele Secrets?*

3. In terms of the relationships in the book, which seemed most successful to you and why? Which relationships seemed doomed to fail and why?

4. If you could find the "whole story" behind one family mystery, what story would you like to unravel?

5. If you could meet one of your ancestors, which person would you want to meet and why?

If you'd like me to come meet with your group, I'd *love* that. Please contact me through andilit.com.

51865934R00130

Made in the USA
Charleston, SC
04 February 2016